fritters and fatality

Snow Falls Alaska Cozy - 2

wendy meadows

Majestic Owl Publishing LLC
P.O. Box 997
Newport, NH 03773

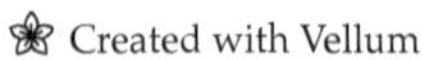 Created with Vellum

chapter one

A warm fire played in an old stone fireplace connected to a rugged, Alaskan cabin sitting on a narrow two-lane road surrounded by nothing except frozen, untamed wilderness that seemed to stretch forever in each direction. Bethany Lights knew Alaska was still a wild, dangerous, and very much "untamed" land that lured brave hearts and daring souls into a life of rugged living. While the world below was poisoned with crowded crime-infected cities, traffic jams, overcrowded airports, overpriced resorts, and unhealthy restaurants, Alaska maintained a pure breath of life that whispered over snowcapped mountains, glassy lakes, roaring rivers, and beautiful wilderness that no writer or poet could accurately place words to. Yes. Alaska was free and clean and beautiful —dangerous, yes, but wasn't danger everywhere? Wasn't it more dangerous to be stuck in work-hour traffic in Los Angeles or Atlanta?

"Yes," Bethany whispered to herself as she cuddled up on a brown recliner with a heavy brown blanket and a cup of hot coffee.

Outside the rustic cabin Bethany called home, a heavy snow was dancing with a howling wind that sounded a bit creepy if not downright scary. Bethany was used to the sounds the icy winds made—but deep down she had to admit the winds seemed to come from a very frightening cave that no man dared to enter. "Up here, the world is different...so different."

"Talking to yourself again?" a voice consumed in a thick British accent asked.

"I'm afraid so," Bethany said, smiling. She turned her head and spotted Julie Walsh entering a warm and safe living room that pretty much resembled a 1950s sitcom living room. Julie carried a cup of coffee over to a green couch and sat down. "I would have washed the dinner dishes—"

"You still have a slight fever, love." Julie eyed her new friend with careful attention. "Your fever is down from yesterday."

"I feel fine. Honest." Bethany appreciated Julie's kind care, but she had to admit that cabin fever was setting in. "I've been wearing these pajamas for three days straight. I've already braided my hair a dozen times, and if I do another Sudoku puzzle, I'll go insane."

Julie simply smiled. Living with Bethany was a joy that she had not expected. Bethany got along with Julie as if they were best friends—no, more than best friends...sisters. The relationship that had blossomed between the two women was sudden and powerful, secure and faithful. Julie was amazed at how deeply she had come to care for Bethany. In the deep chambers of a wounded heart, she knew that God had given her a true sister, a sister that she needed.

"Well, I admit that the blue pajamas you're wearing are becoming a little stale," she teased.

Bethany managed to smile. Julie always dressed so... lovely and stylish. Bethany found her own wardrobe to be bland and boring. Julie wore fun pajamas with little smiley faces on them—Bethany wore boring blue pajamas. Ah. Being roommates allowed Bethany to quickly realize just how drab her wardrobe was—a wardrobe that was slowly starting to match her life. While it was true that Bethany had encountered a pack of killers when she first arrived in Snow Falls, the life that followed had slowly dropped into a dull routine. Wake up. Shovel snow. Go to the coffee shop for a few hours. Eat at the diner. Go see her friends at O'Mally's Department Store, come home, cook dinner, go to bed. Getting sick had actually broken up a monotonous boulder that had become perched on Bethany's heart. "If I ever find a man that wants to take me out for dinner, remind me not to wear these pajamas."

"Deal." Julie glanced down at a heavy pink sweater she was wearing, a sweater that complimented lovely black hair. She had to admit, life had become a little…boring…as well. Taking care of a sick friend had stirred a little excitement. When two women fuss over who gets to wash the dinner dishes…well, something is wrong.

"Bethany?"

"Yes?" Bethany asked as she took a sip of delicious, hot coffee.

"Are you…bored?" Julie asked in a hesitant voice as her eyes—beautiful, intelligent eyes—walked around a cozy, warm living room that offered a sweet sense of comfort, security, and safety that Julie desperately hungered for.

"I'm afraid I am," Bethany quickly admitted. "Sarah and Conrad were smart to take Little Sarah and fly down to Los Angeles and see Pete."

"I'm not so sure leaving Amanda in charge of the snack café at O'Mally's was very clever." Julie laughed some. "My cousin cleans an entire buffet within minutes."

Bethany saw a silly, sweet, loving face appear in her mind. Two hungry hands appeared beside the face holding kosher chili dogs. "Yes, Amanda does have an appetite…and she can definitely polish off an entire load of kosher chili dogs in one sitting."

"My limit is three...." Julie took a sip of her coffee, looked toward the stone fireplace, and then let out a little sigh. "Of course, we talked about Amanda's appetite last night too. I'm afraid we are bored, love."

"We can play Scrabble?" Bethany offered.

Julie scrunched up her nose. "No, thank you, love. I'm quite bored with that game."

"To be honest...so am I." Bethany stared at Julie for a second. It was uncanny how much Julie resembled a young Judi Dench. Julie was definitely a beautiful woman. Bethany guessed the woman she saw in the mirror each morning didn't favor an ugly dog. People always insisted that she favored Jane Wyatt—and Jane Wyatt was a beautiful woman. Yet, Bethany never felt beautiful or attractive. She always felt bland and...square. *Up here in Alaska, a woman has to be more concerned with keeping warm than the current fashions. Not that I care about any current fashions. I prefer the 1950s. Sometimes I think I was born in the wrong era.* "I thought about working on my book, but I still have writer's block."

"Yes, I've noticed." Julie walked her eyes around the living room again. "Maybe we need to take a holiday, love?" she asked in a careful voice.

Bethany felt her heart pick up a little. "A vacation would be nice. I'm not getting any foot traffic at my coffee shop. Snow Falls is the middle of what people call the 'Great Ice' and the 'Polar Bear Winds.' A lot of people leave Snow Falls during this time of year and return when spring arrives." Bethany took another sip of coffee. "I've come to love the snow...and it's not the snow that I'm bored with...or Snow Falls. Julie, I truly do love my new home, and I know you do too. I'm simply—"

"Bored," Julie finished for her.

"Yes, bored." Bethany took a quick nosedive. "When I arrived in Snow Falls, I was forced to fight off a pack of killers while trying to...well, trying to understand where I truly belonged, I guess. I was running from a very painful past...as you were. Now that I've survived that awful scene...with the help of my friends, of course...it seems like all I've accomplished is writing a few miserable sentences in a book that is collecting dust and selling a few cups of coffee at a lonely coffee shop."

"You've accomplished more than me, love," Julie insisted. "At least you have a purpose. All I've been doing is going to O'Mally's every day...sweeping the floors...stocking shelves...driving into town to eat the same meal over and over again at the diner. I'm very grateful for my new life here in Snow Falls, and I truly do love it...but—"

"You're bored."

"Very bored," Julie confessed. "I feel as if I need to take a holiday, love. My heart is yearning to get away for a while. But...and this may sound insane, I'm not wanting to get away from the snow or leave Alaska. As a matter of fact, I'm not wanting to go to any city or a place where there is a lot of people."

"Really?" Bethany asked in a shocked voice. Julie nodded. "Julie, I feel the same way. As a matter of fact...." Bethany reached under her blanket and pulled out a tattered old book. "I've been reading all about Alaska in this book," she explained.

Julie eyed the book Bethany held up—*Forgotten Places of Alaska*.

"This book talks about many forgotten places that used to be very popular...mostly old hunting lodges and ski resorts," Bethany explained. "We're both aware of the resort that Amanda and Sarah were going to buy—"

"The resort where they became infected with a deadly virus," Julie pointed out.

"We'll be more careful." Bethany's voice caused Julie's face to transform into a curious expression. "Julie, there's an old ski resort north of us…about two hundred miles north, give or take. The map in this book is very old. Anyway—"

"Uh, love, are you suggesting we buy a ski resort?" Julie asked in a confused voice.

"No, no, of course not." Bethany laughed. "Julie, last week an old man came into my coffee shop. The old man's name was Mr. John Richtore…at least that's what he told me his name was. Anyway, Mr. Richtore said he was on his way north to help his daughter fix up an old ski resort. That's when he showed me this book. Mr. Richtore talked about the ski resort with a great deal of excitement—at his age, I suppose having something to do was exciting. I was a little taken aback that Mr. Richtore was traveling alone. Anyway, to make a long story short, when Mr. Richtore left my coffee shop, he accidentally left his book behind."

"And you decided to read the book."

"Well, I searched the book for a phone number, but then I became interested in reading about the ski resort Mr. Richtore told me about. The following day, I had Sarah help me find a phone number to the resort and made a call. I spoke to a woman named Shelia Vermont. Shelia Vermont claimed to be the daughter of Mr. Richtore." Bethany lowered the book she was holding up. "Shelia and I talked for a while. She told me that she and her husband were attempting to fix up a run-down ski resort but weren't having much luck. They couldn't find anyone willing to travel so far north to work for them, help them make needed repairs, stuff like that."

"Ah…so you want to lend a helping hand?" Julie asked.

"I mentioned that thought to Shelia…well, only after she jokingly asked if I wanted a job," Bethany confessed. "Shelia didn't shy away from the idea of free help. She seemed so sweet and sincere on the telephone. I could call her and… maybe…we could travel north?"

"But how?" Julie asked. "The roads north are very treacherous."

"Snowcats," Bethany said, offering a confident smile. "Shelia explained to me how to get to the ski resort. She and her husband parked their truck at an old hunting lodge and a man who lives at the lodge with his wife took them to the resort on a snowcat. The only problem was, the man who owns the snowcat charges a very high fee and it's nearly a full day's ride from the hunting lodge to the ski resort."

"Very rugged, huh?" Julie asked.

"According to Shelia, the ski resort she and her husband are trying to repair is located in a very rugged location, yes. Very remote, to be perfectly honest. But…maybe that's what we need, Julie? To get away…sweat some…get our backs sore…get a few blisters on our hands."

Julie considered Bethany's offer. "We'll have to wait until the storm that's over Snow Falls passes and the roads are plowed clean for us. Then we'll have to make a run for it before the next storm arrives. And we'll need lots of supplies and extra winter clothing…blankets…," Julie began creating a mental checklist. "Dry, warm socks are a must…."

"Does this mean—?" Bethany began to ask in a hopeful voice.

"Love, I need to go into the kitchen and get a writing pad and a pencil. We're going to need to write down everything we need. I'm a very meticulous woman when it comes to taking a holiday."

"Oh, Julie!" Bethany exclaimed as an excited smile burst across her face. "Thank you. I didn't want to make the trip alone—and I wasn't sure if I was even going to take the trip. I just feel that I have to get away."

Julie took a quick sip of coffee. "Love, you and I are both suffering from cabin fever. I agree with what you told me; maybe going to bed with a sore back is what we need. I'm sure your friend has plenty of work for us. And, as strange as this might sound, the idea of working myself silly at a closed-down ski resort feels…right to me."

"Me too," Bethany confessed. "I—"

Before Bethany could finish, a brown telephone sitting on a lamp table rang. "Can you answer the call?"

"Sure." Julie walked over to the lamp table and answered the incoming call. "Hello?"

"Yes, uh…I'm not sure if I have the right phone number. I'm trying to reach Bethany Lights?" a woman spoke in a nervous voice.

"Oh, yes, Bethany is my roommate. One second, please." Julie held up the telephone. "It's for you, love."

The idea of leaving her cozy spot before the fireplace wasn't appealing. Bethany had to drag herself out from under the warm blanket she was resting under. She trudged over to the phone, still feeling a bit rough, and took the call. "Hello?"

"Bethany, this is Shelia Vermont. We talked—"

"Oh, hello, Shelia," Bethany said in a shocked voice. "My friend and I were actually just talking about you. How wonderful it is that you called. Maybe that's a good sign."

"A sign?" Shelia asked in a confused voice.

"Yes. Julie, my roommate…and my best friend, well, more like a sister…we were just discussing the idea of traveling to your ski resort and helping you and your husband…free labor, remember?" Bethany tensed up a little. Would Shelia still extend a welcoming offer? She wasn't sure.

"Oh, Bethany, that's the reason I'm calling," Shelia said, nearly breaking down in tears. "My husband…he left me here at the resort. He threw up his hands and left."

"What? Are you all right?" Bethany asked in an alarmed voice.

"Oh, yes, I'm fine. I can contact Mr. Stewart to come and get me and my father at any time. The truth is, I'm not leaving, Bethany. This resort is all I have now. I was hoping that maybe…when the weather clears, you might extend a helping hand? I have no one else to turn to. I know we've never met in person, but my father met you and he said you were a very pleasant woman."

Bethany looked at Julie. "Looks like we're traveling north. You better go get the writing pad and pencil. I have a feeling we're about to take a very exciting trip."

What Bethany didn't know as she focused her mind back on Shelia was that a killer was waiting at the ski resort she and Julie were about to travel to.

"Three thousand dollars each!" Bethany could barely believe her ears.

"Round trip," a rugged, grumpy old man that looked meaner than a hungry grizzly bear informed Bethany as he worked on a half-smoked cigar that smelled awful. The old man tossed some cigar smoke out of his mouth and wandered off to a marble fireplace stationed in an old wooden room that smelled of chimney smoke, hard winters, and coffee. "Take it or leave it. Gas ain't free, and neither is my time."

Julie lowered her gaze to a wooden floor that was holding what appeared to be a ton of luggage. "Mr. Stewart, we don't have three thousand dollars in cash, I'm afraid."

"I take checks," Claude Stewart told Julie as he chewed on his cigar. "Wife is in the kitchen making lunch. You can pay for a room, and we can leave out for Ice Mountain tomorrow morning, or you can turn back and drive south before night arrives. Not much daylight this time of year." Claude reached out a pair of hard, rough hands toward a blaring fire. "I don't expect folks to carry cash on them. If Shelia vouches for you, then I'll trust you to write me out a check. If your check bounces, I'll hold Shelia responsible."

Bethany had the money Claude was demanding—and so did Julie. But three thousand dollars wasn't chicken feed. "We've traveled so far already…it would be a shame to turn back. And Shelia was so excited when we called her a few minutes ago and told her we'd arrived here at the hunting lodge." Bethany dropped her shoulders. "All right, Mr. Stewart, I'll pay the fare you're asking for—"

"Bethany, I can—" Julie began to object.

"Julie, I can cover our fare," Bethany promised. "I know you have the money, but I also know money is tight for you at times." Bethany stuffed a pair of hands covered with thick gray winter gloves into the pockets of a heavy blue winter jacket. "We'll be paying to stay the night as well."

"Hundred dollars a night…each," Claude told Bethany. "Money includes three squares and free coffee." Claude glanced over his shoulder at the two women standing in his hunting lodge. "That old ski resort ain't worth your time. Shelia is throwing money into the wind. The ski lifts are rusted beyond repair, the main lodge is a mess, the ski cabins are a mess, wiring is dangerous…place needs to be forgotten about."

"You've been to the ski—" Bethany began to ask.

"Wife and me thought about buying the place ourselves at one time. After I examined everything, I threw my hands up and walked away. The resort ain't worth a penny. Would cost a fortune to fix the place up…even if you had the money to do that, folks ain't gonna come piling in. Ice Mountain is a treacherous mountain. Many folks have died on that mountain. That's why the ski resort was closed in the first place."

"Then why did you think about buying the ski resort yourself?" Bethany asked Claude in a curious voice.

Claude turned his eyes back to the roaring fire he was standing in front of. "I was stupid," he offered an honest answer, "and much younger. Wife wanted me to consider buying the ski resort before we bought this hunting lodge… was more her idea than mine. Reckon love makes a man consider stupid possibilities." Claude shook his head. "If the ski resort was a mess when I looked at it all those years ago, I can't imagine how bad it is now. Shelia's husband was right to leave…but not right to leave his wife. I told him so too."

Julie glanced at Bethany with worried eyes. However, it was far too late to turn back. Besides, Julie had learned to never take a person's word at face value unless her own eyes had seen exactly what the person speaking had actually witnessed. "Well, perhaps we should get settled into your rooms?" she asked.

"Weather will be clear all day tomorrow, but then a storm front will move in. Storm front will clear in about a week or so," Claude explained without showing any interest in walking over to a wooden front counter in order to check Bethany and Julie in. "I'll be leaving here as soon as I take you up on the mountain. Wife and me are going to Fairbanks to visit our daughter. Won't be back for two weeks, which means you'll be staying up on the mountain until we get back."

"My friend and I are planning to stay at the resort for three weeks, Mr. Stewart," Bethany told Claude. *I'm tired. It's been a very difficult trip just to reach this hunting lodge. I'm not in the mood to fuss with a money-hungry old-timer. And after talking to my mother and hearing her complain about my new life…over and over again…why do I even call her…my head is hurting.* Bethany sighed. *I'm free of an abusive marriage. I've braved an unknown land to start a new life. I've survived nearly being killed. I've come too far to give up…and to be nagged by my mother because I'm taking a trip to a closed ski lodge.* "We'll be very grateful if you can pick us up at the set time."

"Just tell me the day you want to leave, and I'll be there if I can," Claude said, his tone casual. It was clear that the two women standing in his lodge were going to the old Ice Mountain Ski Lodge to help a foolish woman and an old man. What was it any of his business? Claude was much too old to care for anything more than chopping firewood and making sure food was on the table.

"Three weeks from tomorrow will be the day we'll need to be picked up, Mr. Stewart."

Bethany glanced around the room she was standing in. Although rugged and very rough in appearance, it did offer a…somewhat…cozy atmosphere. A wooden table holding an old chessboard sat next to a window that was covered over with a deep green drape. Bethany imagined Claude sitting at the table with his wife on a dark, cold winter night playing a game of chess while drinking coffee and munching on a cigar. *Up here the world is different. People want to rule the cities where there's streetlights, traffic, grocery stores, running water…and plenty of crime. Up here in Alaska, the land becomes a court of justice and the winters become a hard jury.*

"Well, we better get checked in. I would like to rest a little before lunch," Julie spoke up, hoping that Claude would accept her hint.

Claude turned and looked at Julie. He saw a very beautiful British woman standing before him wearing a white winter coat and a white ski cap. "You best dress for warmth and not style," he warned Julie. "My hunting lodge sits up high, but Ice Mountain sits even higher. It's cold enough up there to freeze a man's blood. Wind that high up can cut a man in half like a sharp razor blade." With those words spoken, Claude worked on getting Bethany and Julie checked in to two warm rooms and said nothing more, even during lunch and dinner. Bethany and Julie didn't mind. They were both exhausted and went to bed early, falling asleep to the sound of a howling, scary wind.

The following morning, Claude loaded a ton of luggage into the back of an antiquated yellow snowcat that looked rusted and beaten down. While Claude loaded the luggage using a pair of snowshoes to stand on top of a mountain of deep, frozen snow, Bethany and Julie struggled into the back of the snowcat—a small compartment that reminded them of a school bus. Samantha Stewart, Claude's wife, struggled to position herself into a tight front seat. The woman was tough as cat snot and looked meaner than a rattlesnake—yet, she possessed a heart of gold. "Goodness, that wind is awful this morning," Samantha called back to Bethany and Julie. "Claude, hurry up!" Samantha made sure the gray muffler hat she was wearing was firmly clamped down over a set of heavy gray hair.

"I'm hurrying!" Claude griped as he threw Bethany's and Julie's luggage into the back of the snowcat.

Bethany situated herself against a small round window that was soaked with ice. White, heavy streams of water vapor left her mouth with each breath she took. The inside of the snowcat felt colder than the temperature outside. The inside of the snowcat felt unfriendly and harsh—a feeling Bethany was very familiar with. *This snowcat feels like how my husband used to treat me. Yet, I depended on my marriage...like I'm depending on this snowcat.*

Julie stationed herself next to Bethany. She was now decked out in a thick brown winter coat and a brown winter muffler hat that managed to fight off the cold. "It's very beautiful here. The lodge sits in the middle of a white wonderland. And you can hear the river from here and almost see the lake."

"Yes, the land is very beautiful, but dangerous," Samantha cautioned. "Claude, don't forget the food basket. We have a long trip up to Ice Mountain and back!"

"I got the food basket already packed, Sam...stop your fussing at me!" Claude barked.

Samantha rolled her eyes. She was a thin woman, but her hands still packed a good punch; and Claude knew it. "Hurry up and let's get going. We're going to have to stay up on the mountain tonight and then drive back down first thing tomorrow." Samantha quickly wrapped a heavy green blanket over her lap and prepared for a very rough ride. "Hurry up!"

"I'm hurrying!" Claude hollered. "Woman, we've been married forty-three years already…and you still as fussy as a yapping dog!"

Bethany and Julie both giggled some. *Marriage is beautiful…when love is true,* Bethany thought as she hugged her arms over a heavy green coat and waited. *It's freezing, but the cold feels good. I feel…alive. For the first time in so long, I actually feel alive. No matter how hard this trip is going to be, I'm glad Julie and I decided to take it. I need this…I need to be away from the world.* "Mrs. Stewart, can we please have some coffee?"

"Claude, bring me the thermoses I brought out! The thermoses are in the white carry box—"

"I know where the thermoses are at, Sam!" Claude threw a brown suitcase into the back of the snowcat and began grumbling to himself. "Women pack everything but the kitchen sink…blasted females gonna get themselves killed up on the mountain…should have my head examined…."

Twenty minutes later, Claude removed his snowshoes and climbed into a battered gray driver's seat, slammed a rusted door closed, and looked toward a two-story, snow-soaked hunting lodge that now seemed lonely and cold. "I left the water running. The solar generator our daughter forced us to get should hold…all them solar panels her husband paid to have put on the roof seem to be doing all right."

"Sure beats having to use gas all the time…saves us a pretty penny too," Samantha told her husband. "Quit your worrying and let's go. The lodge will be fine. The stove is off, the water is running, the pipes are wrapped real warm, the fireplace is cold, and the firewood is covered up." Samantha handed her husband a white cup full of hot coffee. "Here, warm your insides."

Claude accepted the coffee with a hand that was covered

with a thick black glove. "Well, we best get moving," he decided, taking a sip of coffee. "Hold my coffee until I get us moving."

When Claude brought the snowcat to life, Bethany felt her heart jump. Julie tensed up as well. Heavy, ugly, dark diesel smoke shot out a rusted funnel stationed on the right side of the snowcat. The smoke drifted up through a pair of snow-packed trees like a bad dream slowly vanishing. Claude kicked the gas pedal a few times. The snowcat grumbled and then growled until it settled into a steady rhythm. "Here we go," she whispered to Julie.

"Here we go," Julie echoed, managing a little smile.

"Who wants a donut?" Samantha called out as Claude pushed the snowcat into drive and slowly started to ease the machine forward. Bulldozer-type wheels began crunching over hard, frozen snow.

"Save the donuts," Claude fussed. "Let's get some space between us and the lodge before we gobble down the food." Claude's tone told Bethany that the old man wasn't sure if the snowcat was going to be able to make the trip or not.

"Oh, you always worry that Cat might break down on us, you old fart, but she never does. Now stop your fussing and settle down." Samantha leaned back in her seat and looked through a front window that was in the shape of a large square. Claude kept a tarp over the window, which kept the ice off and saved time having to defrost the window. "Ah, I always enjoy the ride up to Ice Mountain."

Claude mumbled something that Bethany didn't hear. "He's a grumpy one, isn't he?" she whispered to Julie.

"I'm afraid he is," Julie said, grinning.

"I heard that!" Claude snapped. "You two want to walk up to Ice Mountain?"

"Oh, leave them alone." Samantha leaned over and slapped Claude on his arm. "Let's all relax and enjoy the ride."

Bethany and Julie both smiled some and then settled back as the snowcat began moving toward a long, treacherous road that connected to a deadly mountain. *Here we go…we're on our way.* Bethany whispered a silent prayer and then forced her mind to relax and enjoy the scenery.

As Bethany settled back in her seat and the snowcat began to climb up a snow-scarred dirt road, a deadly killer pulled a frozen body into a broken walk-in freezer and then vanished. The body belonged to a dead woman—a woman who was killed by the hands of a vicious killer who was determined to kill anyone else who dared step foot on top of Ice Mountain.

Bethany had no idea that a killer was lurking at the top of Ice Mountain and that a horrible night was waiting to greet her.

"Who wants to sing a song?" Samantha called out.

"No songs!" Claude barked. "Just sit back and…enjoy the scenery!"

Enjoy the scenery. Yes. That's what I'll do, Bethany told herself as the snowcat continued to take her closer and closer to the arms of a hidden killer.

chapter two

The snowcat Claude was driving cautiously pushed along a snowy, icy road that was so narrow Bethany and Julie both were certain they were going to meet their doom. A massive rock wall soaked with ice hugged the left side of the road. Nothing but dark, open, snow-ripped air hugged the right side of the snowcat. Bethany knew that if Claude made one wrong move, the snowcat was going to plunge into a bottomless abyss of misery and death. And to make matters worse, the clear weather that had been soaking a pleasant winter day had been interrupted by an unexpected snowstorm. The snowcat was too far away from the hunting lodge to turn back. The ski lodge loomed closer. Claude had no choice but to keep pushing forward through the storm.

"Can you see all right?" Samantha's worried voice filled the interior of the snowcat.

"Yeah…I can see all right," Claude grumbled. The grumpy old man was hunched forward over a worn-down steering wheel struggling to see. The headlights attached to the snowcat offered very little assistance. Claude had slowed the it down to a crawl, easing forward at the pace of a sleepy turtle. "I'm more worried about the gas. At the rate we're traveling, the cat is going to run out of gas and I'm going to have to refuel, which means we might not have enough gas to get back to the lodge…blasted storm."

"Mr. Stewart, how far are we away from the ski resort?" Julie asked. The poor woman was clutching Julie's right arm with desperate, terrified hands.

"About another seven miles or so. This road we're on will flatten out soon but then start to climb again. Once the road flattens out, we'll go about four miles and then travel two more miles up into the clouds. It's like I told you, the road up to the ski resort is treacherous." Claude spoke without taking his attention off the dangerous road the snowcat was struggling up. Heavy, impossible snow slapped the front windshield, forcing a pair of old windshield wipers to work overtime. "Used to be a decent road that led up to the ski resort back in the older days. The road was pretty much safe. But an earthquake struck this mountain and caused some of the mountain to cave in on the road. State never worked to clear the landslide. A man named Roger Liland managed to build this road we're on. Connected this road to part of the old road that can still be used. Took some doing, so…at least that's what I was told."

"The earthquake put the ski lodge out of business. No one wanted to risk traveling this road," Samantha explained. "I can't blame them."

"Wouldn't be so bad if the landslide could be cleared and the ski resort could be fixed up," Claude grumbled and then shook his head. "Would take an army of machines to clear the landslide…would take at least a year. Even if the landslide was cleared and the road was put back in order, the ski resort is too battered down. You'd have to tear down the entire ski lift, all the old buildings…just clear out the entire resort and build everything new."

"I'm afraid you're right," Samantha agreed while holding on to her seat with firm hands. "I wasn't aware of how dangerous this road was and the awful shape the ski resort was in. I don't even like making this trip…but money is money. No offense," Samantha called back to Bethany and Julie. "You two are darlings, but my husband and I have to earn a living. Danger or no danger, six thousand dollars goes a long way for two old mules like us."

"We're going to be fine," Claude assured his wife. "We've traveled this road with the cat. I know my way."

"It ain't you I'm worried about. We've never traveled this road in the snow before, Claude. I can barely see a foot in front of the cat," Samantha pointed out.

"Well, what do you expect me to do, Sam? Turn back? Impossible. I have to keep the cat moving. You feel how strong the winds are? I have to get up to the top of the mountain and settle down. There's no way we can travel back down in this storm." Claude quickly slipped his right hand into the right pocket of the coat he was wearing and snatched out a half-smoked cigar. "I'll keep us moving."

Bethany looked over at Julie. "Are you all right?"

Julie winced. "All I see is ice on one side of me and a steep drop-off on the other side, love. I'm not going to lie and say I'm prepared to start singing darling little jingles." Julie focused on the back of Claude's head. "Mr. Stewart, I know the weather changed very suddenly and the situation we're in isn't your fault. I know you're doing your best and I have full confidence in you. So please excuse me if I sound like a tattered rag doll that's about ready to wet her pants."

"No need to worry about bothering me," Claude told Julie as he chewed on his cigar like a tough old cab driver. "I'd be lying myself if I said I ain't a bit worried. Ain't got no choice but to keep going, though."

"The things we do for money," Samantha sighed.

"Sam—"

"Well, it's true," Samantha insisted. "Claude, they raised the age of Social Security to sixty-seven. You're sixty-three and I'm sixty-one. We barely get anybody to stay at the lodge.

We live off the money your folks left you before they died... and Claude, you and I both know that money isn't much. We spent our golden egg buying that hunting lodge."

"Our problems are our problems," Claude snapped in a way that told his wife he didn't want two strangers hearing about their financial problems.

"Oh, go fuss to the wind. It's not like Bethany and Julie are going to go blab our problems to the polar bears," Samantha snapped back. "All I'm saying, Claude, is that we scrape and save and fight our way through one hard winter after the next...for what?"

Claude bit down on the cigar in his mouth. "Are you saying you want to leave the lodge?"

"Of course not. That lodge has become my home. I'll be buried next to the lodge someday if Jesus don't come first. All I'm saying is that maybe we should take Max up on his offer and start—"

"No," Claude snapped again in a hard tone. "Sam, Max ain't a bad fella, but his idea to turn our lodge into some Christian marriage retreat center...Sam, I'm a hunter. I take men out to hunt. I don't want to hear a bunch of whiny people crying over their marriages."

Samantha sighed. "Max, that's our daughter's husband, is a pastor," she explained to Bethany and Julie as Claude carefully drove the snowcat forward through a growling snow. "Max suggested we turn the hunting lodge into a kind of...a Biblical marriage retreat place...where people can come and heal their marriages."

"That sounds like a good idea," Julie told Samantha.

Marriage retreats. I can't imagine my dead husband ever wanting to go on a marriage retreat. My husband's idea of showing me any compassion was belittling me with his words. Bethany felt an old, familiar bitterness touch her heart. *No. Now isn't the time to let your heart become angry. You need to focus on reaching the ski lodge.* "Mr. Stewart, I agree that the idea your son-in-law suggested does seem reasonable. Perhaps you can work out a schedule?"

"That's what Max has been telling the stubborn old goat," Samantha exclaimed. "But my husband doesn't want to budge on the matter."

"I just ain't the…mushy type, is all," Claude fussed. "I take men out into the wild who are rough as I am. I'm not going to serve…coffee and donuts…to a bunch of sissy guys who can't control their marriage. And before you ask me what that means, I'll tell you!" Claude bit down on his cigar again. "A man is supposed to control his marriage the way God teaches him to in the Bible. It's as simple as that. A man is supposed to love his wife, put her on a pedestal…but he's also the man of the house. His job is to take care of business and the woman's job is to tend to the house and children. If that sounds old-fashioned…let those who don't like it take the matter up with God."

"Claude, just because a man is having problems with his marriage doesn't mean he's a sweater-wearing sissy," Samantha insisted.

"Then you tell me why a fella would travel all the way to our lodge to sit in a circle with other guys who can't handle their marriage and talk about their…feelings." Claude rolled his eyes. "In my day, when a man and woman had problems in their marriage, they got on their knees together and prayed the problem out. Nowadays folks want them silly songs… books…movies…to tell them what love is. Well, I'll tell what you love is…." Claude waited until a powerful gust of wind passed before continuing. "Love is committing yourself to your wife for life as a man of God. Love is holding your wife's hair while she's vomiting…taking her toilet paper when she has diarrhea…wiping her tears away after she's given birth to a baby. Love ain't no blasted silly song and a bunch of mushy feelings. That's why I don't agree with Max! The thought of a bunch of diaper-wearing men sitting around with their wives talking about their…feelings…turns my stomach!"

Bethany felt a tender grin touch her mouth. *Claude may be rough around the edges, but I have to admit, he tells it like it is.* "Well, maybe you can be out in the woods when a marriage retreat is taking place, Mr. Stewart?" Bethany knew her suggestion was pretty foolish, but she felt the need to offer some support to Samantha.

"Maybe I should go dance with a wild grizzly bear too," Claude snapped. "Bah…drop the subject. I got to focus on the road."

Samantha sighed. "Claude…oh, forget it. You're as hardheaded as your old man was."

"My old man was hard, but he did what God expected of him, and he did right by my mother and me and my two sisters. Never went hungry once. Went to school. Went to church every Sunday. Read my Bible every night before bed. Said my prayers every day. My old man raised me right."

"Yeah, he did," Samantha nodded. "Ned was a good man…stubborn, but he was a good man." Samantha focused on the front windshield. "How much longer before we hit the straight stretch?" she asked, changing the topic.

"About another half mile…" Claude narrowed his eyes. "Snow is coming down harder. Once we hit the stretch, I'm going to have to gain some speed. I don't want to stop and fill up the tank with the gas that's meant to get us back to the lodge, Sam." Claude glanced at a rusted old fuel gauge. "We should arrive at the ski resort on fumes if I manage our gas right. There ain't no place to turn around, not even on the straight stretch. We're on a one-way trip to the ski resort. Only place I'll be able to turn the cat around is at the ski resort."

Bethany looked out a small window to her left. All her eyes managed to see was a snowy, dark ice wall. "Coming back down the mountain should be fun," she said, trying to joke with Julie a little.

"I think I'll walk." Julie tried to laugh some but failed. "Love, I think we should come back down the mountain with Mr. and Mrs. Stewart. You see how dangerous this road is. I think if you and I had known this road was so dangerous, we would have remained in Snow Falls. I honestly can't say that I see any point in helping your friend try to get an old ski resort in tip-top shape when…the idea of hope seems very remote."

Bethany slowly folded her arms together. "I've been considering the same truth from the moment Mr. Stewart began taking us up this road. Shelia told me the road up to the ski lodge was treacherous, but not this treacherous. I think when we get to the ski resort, we'll explain to Shelia our feelings and then leave with Mr. and Mrs. Stewart."

"No refunds," Claude called out.

"Oh, of course," Bethany assured Claude. "Mr. Stewart, Julie and I wouldn't dare ask for a refund. You and Mrs. Stewart are very brave to have taken us this far." *I sound like a pathetic old mule. I'm always so nice. Why can't I simply just say what I'm thinking? Why am I always afraid of offending others when others aren't afraid of offending me? I have a bad feeling Julie is the same way I am.*

"That's very kind of you, Bethany," Samantha said in a grateful voice. "I can tell you have a good heart…and so does Julie. I'm glad to hear that you two will be coming back down the mountain with us. I'm sorry you wasted your time and… money, but you sure helped me and my husband."

"Mrs. Stewart, maybe Julie and I can stay at your lodge and take our vacation there?" Bethany suggested.

"That would be nice," Julie agreed. "Who knows? Maybe we'll run into a couple of handsome lumberjacks?"

Samantha laughed. "You'll have a better chance of running into a hungry grizzly bear."

"We're supposed to be going to see Gennifer—" Claude began to object.

"Oh, Gennifer can wait," Samantha fussed. "You know as well as I do Max is behind the visit. Max wants to talk more about his idea, Claude. And since you're so set against Max's idea, what's the rush to get to Fairbanks?"

Claude chewed on his cigar. "Hundred dollars a night... three square meals provided," he grumbled.

Bethany couldn't help but to smile. Julie joined her. Claude was an old fuss, but he was the type of old fuss that Bethany and Julie were becoming fond of. "Deal," Bethany told Claude.

"We'll be staying for two weeks, Mr. Stewart. By the time Bethany and I leave for Snow Falls, I'm sure we will have accomplished driving you insane. As a matter of fact, Bethany and I will make that task our sole duty," Julie told Claude and then laughed some. Why not? Laughter was good for the heart.

Claude looked over at Samantha. Samantha simply smiled and focused back on the storm. Claude nodded and continued to cautiously drive the snowcat up a treacherous, dangerous road toward a deadly ski resort that was hiding a vicious killer.

We made it. We've made it to the ski resort safe and alive. My mother would be pouring gravy into her lap right now if she knew the road I just traveled up. She would have a bunch of men carrying butterfly nets start chasing me. Bethany wiped a little nervous sweat off her brow as Claude churned the snowcat she was traveling in through a narrow, icy gap of rock that eventually opened up into the mouth of an icy, snow-scarred mountain. But instead of seeing a lovely, cozy, and inviting ski resort appear before her eyes, all Bethany managed to see was heavy snow.

"We're running on fumes, but we're here," Claude spoke in a relieved voice. "The ski lodge is just ahead about half a mile. We'll just have enough gas." Claude checked the gas gauge once again and then pressed down on a stubborn gas pedal. The snowcat lurched forward, gaining a little speed as it moved down a snowy trail surrounded by frozen white trees. "Only way in and out of the resort is through the rock gap," Claude explained. "As for the snowcat, if you're on foot, you'll have to hike north past the high rocks and then swing back around south…takes about a full day unless you got climbing gear to climb over the high rocks."

"Claude has a million maps," Samantha explained, a deep hint of relief in her voice as her husband continued to drive the snowcat toward a beaten-down ski lodge. "He knows the land by heart."

"No man can truly know the land," Claude cautioned. "Respect the land and you'll do fine."

Bethany and Julie both remained quiet until the headlights attached to the snowcat splashed onto a wooden building that resembled a creepy horror house. The ski lodge didn't resemble any cozy ski lodge Bethany had ever seen. Usually ski lodges were…well, cozy and inviting. The ski lodge that appeared in the headlights of the snowcat looked more like a creepy two-story lake cabin that housed a few hidden monsters—monsters Bethany didn't want to be introduced to. "No lights in the lodge—"

"I see," Claude told his wife before the woman could finish her sentence. He slowly eased the snowcat to a stop in an area that had once been a gravel parking area. With skilled eyes, he examined the ski lodge. Shelia lived in the ski lodge in a small upstairs apartment that had been built for the ski resort's manager to reside in with his family. Claude wasn't sure why the entire downstairs area of the ski lodge was dark, and why couldn't he spot a light up on the second floor?

"I best go take a look."

"I'm coming with you," Samantha insisted. "The winds are so strong the cat is being rocked back and forth like a wave in a hurricane. We all need to get inside, Claude."

Claude knew his wife was right. "All right," he said in a stern voice, turning in his seat, "here's the game plan. We'll leave the luggage for now. I've got my gun tucked into the pocket of my coat. My hunting rifle is in the back…that's all we're taking for now. We need to get inside the lodge and find Shelia and her old man. We'll worry about the luggage later—"

"Mr. Stewart, you can leave our luggage. We're not staying," Bethany reminded Claude.

Claude nodded. He wanted to make double sure Bethany and Julie were going back down the mountain in the snowcat. Women were fickle creatures. "Then let's move." Without saying another word, Claude disengaged his seat belt. He didn't need to tell Samantha to open a rusted glove compartment and take out a green flashlight. Samantha was a mountain gal. The woman knew how to think on her feet. Claude was worried that Bethany and Julie might have opposing minds and turn out to be flapping fish instead of strong reindeer.

Bethany waited as Claude climbed out into the snowstorm, still chewing on a half-smoked cigar. "Well… ready?" she asked Julie.

"We've come such a long way…and we're so far away from the world. Perhaps that's why I'm feeling a bit creepy and scared right now, love…or maybe…." Julie nodded toward the ski lodge. Claude had left the headlights attached to the snowcat on. The headlights were fighting through a heavy snow, struggling to give light to the creepy building. "I suppose I didn't expect our holiday to turn out like this. I suppose I expected a cozy ski resort that needed some repairs and a little dusting."

Bethany leaned forward in her seat. She eyed the ski lodge with a worried, pessimistic frown. *I have to admit, the ski lodge is very creepy in appearance. Of course, this ski lodge was built in the year 1953, according to the book I was reading.* Bethany sighed. *I moved to Snow Falls to create a new life for myself. I bought a cabin and a coffee shop…and now look at me…I'm sitting on top of a dangerous mountain looking at a creepy ski lodge that needs to be torn down. My life in Alaska isn't exactly turning out to be all sunshine and roses.*

The sound of Claude opening up the back of the snowcat caused Bethany to jump a little. "All right, got my rifle," Claude called out over a howling, icy—deadly—wind. "Everyone out. Let's get inside!"

"Let's go, girls!" Samantha quickly turned off the snowcat's headlights, clicked on the flashlight, and shouted, "Follow me!"

"Stay close," Bethany whispered to Julie.

"Like glue," Julie promised.

Bethany nodded and then helped Julie out of the snowcat. The two women worked their way out into a blazing snowstorm screaming through a viciously dark night. Both Bethany and Julie immediately sank down into snow that was up to their knees. "Oh my!" Julie called out.

Bethany quickly grabbed Julie's arm with her right hand and shielded her eyes from the winds with her left hand. She tried to look around, but all she saw was a veil of darkness snapping at her through the snow. *I feel like I'm in the mouth of an insane killer,* she thought as Samantha aimed the flashlight she was holding toward the ski lodge. *Or maybe that's simply the writer in me. I did write a book that had the…perfect murder in it.*

"Let's go!" Claude yelled over the winds in a fussy tone. "No sense in standing out here freezing to death!"

"I'm standing in snow up to my knees and he wants me to hurry," Julie told Bethany in a painful voice.

Samantha reached out and took Julie's hand. "Come on, we'll trudge through the snow together!" Samantha threw a set of worried eyes around. "Bethany, hold Julie's arm just like you're doing. We'll move like a choo-choo train…holding on to each other. Claude, lead the way!"

Claude nodded and began working his way through the deep snow carrying his rifle in an offensive firing position. If something was wrong inside the lodge, Claude was prepared to shoot and ask questions later. Perhaps a hungry grizzly bear had somehow wandered down to the lodge? A pack of wolves? Claude wasn't certain why the ski lodge was dark as he fought his way through the storm. The last thing his trained mind ever assumed was that a deadly killer was on the loose.

When Claude reached a heavy entry door attached to the ski lodge, he carefully reached out a gloved hand and tried a rusted doorknob. To his relief, the doorknob turned. "Follow me inside…slowly now…Sam, keep that flashlight over my shoulder."

Samantha pushed her way through the deep snow until she was nearly standing on Claude's heels. She aimed the flashlight in her gloved hands over the man's shoulders. Claude nodded, checked his rifle, and then pushed the entry door open. The door in question had been built to withstand powerful winds and cruel winters. The screaming winds battering Bethany, Julie, Samantha, and Claude attacked the door but failed to burst the door open. Claude decided he'd have to put his shoulder to the door. When the door was finally open, he stepped into a dark room with his rifle at the ready. Samantha stepped in behind him holding a flashlight with one hand and Julie's hand with her other hand. She quickly scanned a large, open room holding a large stone fireplace and run-down, dusty furniture.

"Claude?" she whispered.

"Give me the light." Claude took the flashlight his wife was holding as Bethany stepped through the entry door. "Leave the door open," he ordered, speaking into a dark, cold room that should have had a large fire going in the stone fireplace and a few lanterns or candles set about. A tall, secured stack of firewood was resting next to the stone fireplace in a tall holder that had been carved into a stone wall. Claude eyed the firewood and then scanned the dark room, turning around in a careful, slow motion. He stopped on a set of wooden stairs that connected the first floor to the second floor. "There's a line of small cabins outside...twenty in total, if I recall...and there's a few guest rooms upstairs... ten, I think...and a small apartment," Claude spoke, keeping his voice low. "Shelia and her husband moved into the apartment. Her old man took one of the guest rooms upstairs. He left not soon after...returned a few weeks ago."

The tone of Claude's voice and his refusal to let the entry door be closed sent a deep worry spiraling down into Bethany's heart. *Mr. Stewart is worried. He's whispering as if he's worried someone might be listening or watching us. Why? And where is Shelia and her dad? Why is the lodge so dark? Why isn't there a fire going?* "Maybe we should check upstairs, Mr. Stewart? Something could have happened to Shelia and her dad."

Claude glanced back toward Samantha. "You feeling it?" he asked.

Samantha nodded yes. "Something is wrong, Claude. We need to fill up the cat and start moving back down the mountain." Urgency ripped Samantha's voice. The woman knew well enough when something was wrong—deadly wrong. "The fireplace hasn't been used all day. This room is colder than the worry running down my spine. Something is wrong."

"Yep." Claude aimed the flashlight he was holding back

toward the wooden staircase. "Can't leave without trying to find Shelia and her old man first, Sam. Would be cowardly of me. You take Bethany and Julie back to the cat and wait for me."

"Mr. Stewart," Bethany spoke up before anyone else could, "we better stay together and not separate. There's power and safety in numbers."

"She's right, Claude," Samantha insisted. "We need to stay together. Something bad has happened. I feel it in my bones."

"I agree," Julie added. "If something is wrong...and I agree with everyone that it certainly seems that something is amiss...I think we should remain connected as a team and watch after each other with careful eyes." Julie's thick British accent waivered a little. The poor woman was simply... downright scared. The room she was standing in felt more like a crypt rather than a cozy lodge—a very creepy crypt.

"I can't be responsible for your safety, ladies," Claude informed Bethany and Julie. "Who knows what's going on? Maybe a hungry bear woke up...seen it happen before. Maybe a pack of wolves got at the place? Seen that happen before too. Not sure what's going on...but it ain't food."

"Mr. Stewart," Bethany told Claude in a firm tone, "from this moment forward, we're not two...customers. We're friends that are going to take care of each other. If anything happens, then at least we'll be able to help each other...no matter the risk. Okay?"

"Bethany is right," Julie told Claude before he could answer. "We're going to take care of each other like a...family. So please don't object or argue."

Claude felt a sense of admiration and respect form in his heart toward Bethany and Julie. Maybe the two women weren't going to turn out to be flapping fish after all. "Then let's get upstairs and have a look around. If we don't find anyone, we'll march straight to the cat, fill her with gas, and turn back."

"That's a plan." Samantha shot Bethany and Julie a smile of gratitude. "You two girls are going to become like my own daughters. I can tell you that's going to happen right now."

Julie squeezed Samantha's hand. "I hope so, love."

"Me too," Bethany managed to smile—a smile that quickly faded. *Why hasn't the fireplace been used? Why is this room so dark and cold? Where is Shelia and her dad? What's going on?* "All right, Mr. Stewart—"

"Best call me Claude if we're going to be family," Claude told Bethany and then eyed the wooden stairs. "All right, let's get upstairs and have a look around. I'm not sure what we might find…might not find a thing. Then again, we might find Shelia and her dad in a bad way. Best prepare yourselves for that right now."

Bethany and Julie glanced at each other with worried eyes and then nodded their heads. Samantha drew in an uneasy breath. "Let's go," she ordered. "If anyone hears or sees anything, holler out and Claude will start shooting."

Claude ordered everyone to stand close to his back. Once everyone was in place, he carefully moved toward the wooden stairs, glanced up into a cloud of darkness, and then handed Samantha back the flashlight. "Keep the flashlight over my shoulder. I'll need both hands to shoot with if needed."

Samantha took the flashlight back from her husband, looked around, and then waited as Claude checked his rifle one last time. "Ready?" she asked.

Claude nodded. "Let's go."

Bethany and Julie watched as Claude bravely began to climb up the wooden stairs. The stairs began to creek and moan under his feet like screaming nightmares—at least that's what Bethany's mind heard. "Stay close, girls," Samantha whispered as she began to follow her husband up the stairs.

Bethany and Julie both drew in a deep breath and

followed Claude and Samantha up the stairs. As they did, a shadowy figure appeared outside in the storm. Moving on quick legs, the figure located a full red can of gas that was sitting in a metal cage attached to the left side of the snowcat.

"No one is leaving this ski resort alive," the figure whispered as it removed the can of gas from the cage and vanished back into the snowstorm without being seen or heard, leaving the snowcat stranded. "No one is leaving the ski resort alive…ever."

chapter three

ethany crept down a long, dark hallway that creaked and moaned under every step. The hallway had a line of closed doors attached to it like a splinter from a piece of a broken bone. Wooden numbers that sat at uneven angles rested on each closed door. At the end of the hallway, a closed door appeared. Behind the closed door stood a set of wooden stairs that led up to a small apartment. *I'm sure at one point in time this ski resort might have appeared welcoming and even attractive…but now this place resembles a spooky graveyard. I wish I would have never suggested taking this trip. Poor Julie. She's so scared…and so am I. How will she ever trust me again?*

"Stay close," Samantha called back over her shoulder. "Julie, don't let go of Bethany's hand. She's taking up the rear."

"I've got her hand," Julie assured Samantha. "I've also got your hand. I'm not letting go. I promise."

Claude didn't look back. He kept scanning each closed door he walked past with careful eyes until he reached the closed door at the end of the hallway. Bethany watched as Claude quickly reached out his left hand and tried the door. "Locked," he announced. "The door swings out and not in…I can't kick it open. I'll have to remove the door from its hinges...I have a toolbox in the cat."

Samantha scanned the closed door with the flashlight she was holding. "Claude, you know as well as I do that sometimes the Good Lord has a way of saying 'no.' I think this is one of those times. Let's get back to the cat and leave this place."

Bethany expected Claude to object. Instead, the man simply nodded. "Yeah, the bad feeling sitting in my gut is growing worse by the second. Let's go." Instead of calling out anyone's name—which is something Bethany might have done—Claude turned away from the closed door and began walking back down the hallway at a steady pace.

"Let's hurry, girls," Samantha urged, remaining very close to her husband.

Bethany threw a quick eye at the closed door. Was Shelia and her dad up in a hidden apartment hurt...or even worse... dead? Bethany didn't know. All she knew was that Claude was right: it was time to leave. Something was horribly wrong. *This feeling is worse than the one that haunted me in Snow Falls when I had to face a pack of killers. At least I was in Snow Falls where there was electricity...light...and life. This place feels like an empty tomb.* Bethany tore her eyes away from the closed door and began back down the hallway, holding tightly to Julie's gloved hand. *I need to remain calm and functional. I don't need to let fear cripple me. I survived nearly being killed in Snow Falls by forcing myself to think...I need to do the same here.*

Claude led everyone back downstairs and back outside into the storm without missing a beat. Once everyone was outside, he pulled the entry door closed and began fighting his way back toward the snowcat. "Get inside the cat," he yelled over a current of screaming, icy winds that were lashing out with vicious claws. "I'll tend to the gas!"

"No, we stay together!" Samantha hollered back. "I'll hold

the flashlight while you fill the cat with gas. Bethany and Julie can keep an eye out for us."

Bethany trudged through knee-deep snow until she reached the snowcat. She paused just in time to see Samantha aim the flashlight she was holding at the cage attached to the side of the snowcat—the cage that held a large can of reserve gas. Bethany had watched Claude place a large red can of gas into the cage before leaving the hunting lodge. She had watched the man chain the can of gas in place and then secure the cage. *The can of gas…it's missing!* Bethany wasn't certain if she cried out her words in her mind or actually spoke them.

"What in the world…?" Claude dashed forward toward the cage. "No…."

Samantha froze in her tracks as the light from the flashlight in her hand clearly gave life to an empty, rusted cage. "Claude?" she managed to call out over the screaming winds as painful snow pelted her face.

Claude slung his rifle over his right shoulder. "No!" he yelled as his free hands began to work open the empty cage. A simple lock secured the cage—a lock any two-year-old could open. Claude never saw a need to buy a stronger lock. He lived out in the middle of the Alaskan wilderness in a hunting lodge with his wife. Who would want to steal a can of gas off his snowcat except a bear or a moose?

"Bethany?" Julie asked in a panicked voice. "The reserve gas…it's missing." Julie's voice barely carried over the icy winds. "Someone stole the gas…."

Claude slammed the cage door closed with furious hands. "We're on fumes…we don't have enough gas to go another three miles at most. I know the cat…I know how far she can go!" he hollered over the winds. "Without the gas, we're stranded."

"Everyone get inside the cat," Samantha yelled in a panicked voice.

Samantha didn't have to ask twice. Bethany grabbed

Julie's hand and pulled her scared friend back into the snowcat as quickly as she could. Claude fought his way around the front of the snowcat and managed to climb back into the driver's seat. Samantha crashed into the front passenger seat and slammed a rusted door closed.

"What's going on?" Julie asked, struggling to speak without sounding overly panicked.

"I don't know," Claude answered through gritted teeth. "Somebody stole the reserve gas can…but why?"

"Are you sure the cat can't take us no more than three miles?" Samantha asked Claude as she locked the front passenger door.

"We'll be blessed to make it three miles, Sam. I really rode the cat dry getting us up here." Claude examined the hunting rifle he was holding. "We'll freeze to death by morning if we try to stay in the cat all night." Claude nodded toward the front windshield. "Can't even see out anymore. Snow has the windshield covered over. Cat will be buried in snow come morning too."

"Are you suggesting we go back inside?" Bethany asked. The idea of going back into the creepy lodge seemed insane.

"We'll freeze by morning. We need to go back inside the lodge and start a fire," Claude explained in a voice that didn't exactly offer a lot of comfort. "We'll hunker down in the front room of the lodge and come morning…well, all we can do is walk out of here."

"Walk…Claude, we're so far up, and we only have one pair of snowshoes in the cat." Samantha looked at her husband with eyes that were fighting to remain calm and strong. "The winds will tear us in half before we get a mile down the mountain."

"We'll have to dress with as much clothes as we can… keep our heads covered mighty good…and tough the walk—"

"But there's no way we'll make it back to the lodge before

night falls again. Once the sun sets, the temperatures become deadlier than a wild snake." Samantha felt a heavy blanket of despair cover her heart. Yes. She was a tough woman who had fought her way through many harsh winters—but she was also a woman who had common sense. Without gas for the snowcat, there was no chance of leaving the mountain…alive.

"Wait…Bethany, didn't you call your friend?" Julie asked in a quick voice.

"That's right!" Bethany exclaimed. "Shelia told me the old phone lines that were run to this ski resort still worked. We need to go back inside and find the telephone—"

"They ain't no telephone up here," Claude cut Bethany off in a confused voice. "Shelia had a communication CB radio that broke—told her last time I was up here to fix the radio." Claude turned in his seat. "I ain't much for asking questions…but how did you two come to know about Shelia, anyhow? I done went and assumed in my mind you knew the woman on a personal basis."

"We've never met the woman in person," Bethany confessed. "Claude, Shelia's dad visited the coffee shop I own in Snow Falls. He told me about this ski resort and even pointed it out in a book he had with him." Bethany bit down on her lower lip. "Mr. Richtore was the old man's name. When Mr. Richtore left my coffee shop, he forgot his book. I began reading the book. I came across the ski resort and had a friend help me locate a phone number associated with the resort. My intention was to call Mr. Richtore and tell him that I had his book. I ended up speaking with Shelia—"

"That can't be," Claude insisted. "They ain't no phone lines up this far. The landslide from the earthquake I told you about on the way up the mountain took out the phone lines. Ain't no cell phone service, either, this far up. Shelia hasn't been off this mountain in months. Ain't no way you talked to her by phone."

"Claude is right, Bethany," Samantha cut in. "The last time we were up on this mountain was a few weeks ago. We came up here to get Shelia's husband and drop off her old man. The timing was actually...well, prefect, to be honest. Anyway, Bethany, there's no phone that works—"

"But that's impossible. I called Shelia in Snow Falls and made arrangement to travel to this ski resort with Julie." *What in the world is going on? Am I going crazy? I know I spoke to Shelia Vermont.* "As a matter of fact, Shelia called me on the same day Julie and I agreed to travel to the ski resort."

"I'm telling you they ain't no telephone!" Claude barked. "They ain't no telephone or radio up here...and if I had any sense, I would have put a radio in the Cat before we left, but I didn't. My own radio don't carry good this far up. The radio Shelia has was pretty worthless even when it was working."

"Girls," Samantha began in a calm voice, "I'm not sure if you two realize just how far out in the unknown we are. Just because a few dummies put the Good Lord's world on a map don't mean a hill of beans. Alaska is a world of its own, and this ski resort sits at the top of a dangerous mountain that is a world of its own. You two saw how long it took us to get from the lodge to this mountain in the cat. It's nearing midnight, and we left the lodge right when it turned first light."

Claude eyed Bethany and Julie with hard eyes and then turned back around in his seat. "Sam, somebody went and stole the reserve gas can. We're stranded. We ain't got no choice. Come morning, we're going to have to walk out of here or die trying. It's as simple as that."

"Maybe whoever stole the gas can doesn't want us to leave?" Bethany suggested in a troubled voice. "If we were meant to leave, I think the gas can would have been left untouched."

Samantha's chest tightened. She had not considered the idea that someone stole the gas can with the intention to cause further harm...or death. "Claude—"

"I've got a box full of bullets for my rifle and a full clip for my gun." Claude grew silent for a minute, trying to think about what steps to take next. "If we stay in the cat, we'll freeze by morning. We need to get inside and make a fire… but whoever stole the gas can is surely lurking about…but not in the storm. Don't matter who you are, no one can survive for long walking about in this storm."

"What do we do?" Julie asked in a voice that was obviously very scared. Amanda, Julie's crazy cousin, might have asked for a kosher chili dog to lighten up the situation— and even though Julie did have a sense of humor that she barely showed, she wasn't in the mood to put on a blindfold and eat her last kosher chili dog.

"We have to go back inside," Claude spoke in a reluctant voice. "The upstairs apartment is the only other part of the ski lodge that has a fireplace. Shelia showed me the apartment, but I don't feel like barricading myself in no apartment. Someone might try to burn us down. We could hunker down in one of the ski cabins, but those cabins don't have no firewood. We're going to need heat. The main room in the lodge is our only choice."

"But if we light a fire, we'll become sitting targets," Samantha worried.

"Yep…" Claude gripped his rifle. "Sam, you know as well as I do we'll be dead before first light if we don't get near a warm fire. My body is already so cold I'm starting to ache."

"Me too," Samantha confessed. "My feet are frozen solid."

"Mine too," Julie added.

"I hate to admit it, but my coat…gloves…muffler hat… aren't doing much to keep me warm," Bethany finished. *My ears feel like two icebergs attached to my head. We won't survive long sitting in this snowcat.*

"There's one more option," Claude told everyone. "Could be someone else has a snowcat around and needed our gas. There is the old back trail…the trail is far more dangerous than the road we came up on, but not impossible, I guess. I don't know. Maybe whoever stole the gas is long gone?"

Samantha turned her head and looked into her husband's face. Claude appeared dark and shadowy. "Do you really believe that?" she asked.

Claude shook his head no. "My gut is telling me that Bethany is right. Whoever stole the gas doesn't want us leaving, Sam." Claude checked his rifle. "Well, we either work our way back inside or sit here and freeze to death. When I was in the Marines, I learned the hard way that sometimes you have to face the enemy head-on."

Bethany and Julie grew very silent and listened to the storm pound the snowcat with furious hands. What else could they do? Panicking was not an option—or was it?

So far so good. No sign of anyone—not even Shelia or her dad, assuming Shelia Vermont is actually here at the ski resort. I spoke to a woman who identified herself as Shelia Vermont and a woman who claimed to be Shelia Vermont called my cabin. If I didn't speak to Shelia Vermont…and if Shelia Vermont didn't call me, which it's obvious she didn't…couldn't…then who did I speak to? Bethany stepped close to a warm fire Claude had started in a cold, stone fireplace. The fire offered some warmth and comfort but did very little to fully light up the dark room everyone was standing in. At least there was a fire. A fire represented life and hope—well, the warmth and light of the fire, at least. Anything was better than standing in a cold darkness.

"Claude, maybe we should search for some candles or a lantern? Samantha will need to preserve the batteries in the flashlight."

Claude hated to admit it, but Bethany had a good point. The fire he had started did fight off the darkness some, but not very much. The front room was too large for fire to give light to. There were just too many blasted crooks and crannies. What worried Claude the most was a closed door sitting at the end of the room. The door opened up into a large dining room area. Claude had explored the dining room along with a medium-sized kitchen attached to it. If anyone was sneaking around in the ski lodge, the dining room area, kitchen, front office, the second-floor apartment, or one of the guest rooms offered plenty of good hiding places.

"We need to check the lodge," Claude spoke in a stern tone. "We need to check the front office that sits just behind that counter over there." Claude nodded toward a long wooden counter that stood off in the distance. "We need to check the dining room and the kitchen area and then go upstairs and check the guest rooms and the manager's apartment. I don't like standing around not knowing who might or might not be in the lodge."

"Can't we just stay right here?" Julie pleaded in a desperate voice.

"And do what?" Claude asked Julie as he threw a heavy log into a fireplace that was holding a fire that was slowly gaining life and strength. The glow of the fire washed his face with worried lines. "Someone went and stole the reserve gas can from the cat, Julie. That person might still be around… most likely that person *is* still around. Could be more than one person too. Remember that I only brought Shelia's husband down from this mountain. Shelia and her old man stayed behind. Fussed at them to leave…they refused." Claude shook his head. "Blasted hardheaded mules."

Bethany looked around the front room. Her eyes locked on to three old green and red couches that had been placed in comfortable locations, a dozen green sitting chairs that appeared like boney thumbs in the darkness, a few wooden tables, and the fireplace. The front counter standing off in the distance seemed bare. A door behind the front counter stood closed. Bethany stood very still and listened as her eyes walked around. For a few seconds, she thought she heard the sound of laughter, hot cups of coffee, and hot chocolate being drunk, soft music playing…the sounds of an old ski lodge filled with happy people snuggling up to a warm fire as a hard snow dropped outside. *I suppose there was a time when this ski lodge was very cozy and welcoming…full of adventure, fun…and romance. What once was has become a creepy tomb. Like a thriving mall that becomes deserted. All that is left behind is an empty tomb filled with forgotten skeletons.*

"Bethany?"

"Huh?" Bethany's eyes took her to Julie's worried face. "Yes, Julie?"

"Are you all right, love?" Julie asked in a worried voice. "Your eyes seemed to have…trailed off a bit."

"Oh…I…was just thinking about how…oh, it's not important." Bethany bit down on her lower lip. "I agree with Claude. I think we do need to explore the lodge and make sure we're secure. As of now, we seem to be safe…which makes me wonder what's going on. Is someone watching us? If so, why did that person steal the reserve gas can and then let us find our way back into the lodge and start a fire? Was Claude right in suggesting maybe the person who stole the gas needed gas for another snowcat that might be hidden somewhere?" Bethany shook her head. "I don't know. I don't even know who I spoke to on the telephone…."

Julie looked toward the front counter. An old brown telephone was the only item that sat on the counter. The phone…was dead. Claude had been correct in claiming the ski resort lacked phone service. "Who did you talk to if not Shelia Vermont?" she asked herself more than Bethany.

"We can ask a bunch of questions later. Right now, we need to secure the lodge." Claude took his rifle off a tired shoulder and checked it. "Okay, here's how we're going to work this. Sam, you're coming with me. Bethany, you and Julie are going to stay right here with the fire and keep it going." Before anyone could object, Claude reached under the thick winter coat he was wearing and pulled out a solid Glock 17. "My daughter bought me this gun a few years back as a present. Didn't think I'd like it, but the gun shoots good. Here, take it." Claude held out the gun toward Bethany.

Bethany looked at Julie and then reluctantly accepted the gun. She had mentioned to Claude that she had spent time learning how to fire a gun at a firing range. *Me and my big mouth.* "Claude—"

"Take the gun off safety and shoot," Claude ordered Bethany. "Don't hesitate. If I hear any shooting, I'll come running with Sam. We don't have time to stand around and jabber." Claude scanned the front room and then hurried his eyes over to the closed dining room door. "Sam, we'll check the dining room and kitchen first and then work our way upstairs."

Samantha felt very tense, but she trusted her husband. Claude knew how to track a grizzly bear in his sleep. If someone was hiding in the lodge somewhere, Claude would find that person. "All right. I'm ready."

"You two stay right here next to the fire. Work as a team. Bethany, you watch all the doors and windows, and Julie, you watch the stairs. If you see anyone other than me and Sam… Bethany, shoot first and ask questions later. I'll do the same. If you hear me shoot my rifle, come running. Understand?" Claude demanded.

Bethany began to feel a tender love toward Claude. Yes, Claude was grumpy and ornery, but the man had a deep, caring—and wise—heart beating inside of his spirit. "Shoot first and ask questions later. I understand," she promised. "And I'll take care to watch how many bullets I have."

"Good girl." Claude wasn't sure if handing over his gun to Bethany was smart or not, but there was no way he was leaving two scared ladies unarmed. He studied Bethany's eyes in the glowing fire and then nodded. Bethany was scared, but her eyes told Claude she was a smart woman. "Let's go, Sam. Keep the flashlight over my shoulder and stay close. If you see—"

"If I see anyone, I'll holler," Samantha promised her husband.

Claude nodded, scanned the front room again, and then walked toward the closed dining room door with Samantha following close behind. Bethany nearly followed but forced her legs to remain still. She helplessly watched as Claude and Samantha cautiously eased into a dark, cold dining room with only the light of a weak flashlight to light their way. "He's a brave man."

"He's wonderful," Julie told Bethany, speaking in a sincere tone. "I like the bloke very much...makes me wish he had been my daddy growing up." Julie kept her eyes peeled on the dining room door Claude and Samantha had walked through. Claude had left the door standing open.

"My dad would have become very good friends with Claude," Bethany said in a low voice. *My dad would have never allowed me to make this trip. My dad would have insisted I work out my frustrations in a more sensible manner...and I am frustrated and upset...and so is Julie. We both have a lot of knots sitting in our hearts. Years of an abusive marriage for me...Julie's ex-husband turning her son against her...the brick wall we both hit when we arrived in Snow Falls. Now that I look back, I wonder how we even survived fighting that pack of killers? It all seems like a blur in my mind now...I was very upset and scared...nervous and anxious. Now that I've been able to settle down a bit...I'm being attacked by a new enemy: frustration and anger that's linked to the past...my past.*

"Bethany?"

"Yes?" Bethany asked, keeping her voice low as she scanned the front room with careful eyes.

"I talked to my son before you spoke to me about going on

holiday." Julie's whispering voice was filled with a deep, agonizing pain.

Bethany turned her eyes to Julie. "The conversation didn't go well, did it?"

"No, love, the conversation didn't go well at all," Julie confessed. "My son called me a few harsh names and hung up on me." Julie's heart let out a painful moan. "My son still blames me for putting his dad on 'Poor Street,' as he calls it. I tried to explain to my son that when two people divorce, it's the man's duty to ensure the woman has privileges that will take care of her needs. My son wouldn't listen. I'm the monster, and my ex-husband is the victim."

"I'm sorry, Julie," Bethany offered a sincere truth filled with concern and love. Julie was hurting over her son—a pain only a true mother could feel and…sadly…endure.

"So am I, love," Julie sighed. "Speaking with my son was one of the main reasons I wanted to take a holiday. The idea of traveling to a remote ski resort and earning myself a sore back seemed like the perfect ticket. Hard work always takes my mind off my troubles."

"Hard work can be a friend," Bethany agreed. She reached out with her left hand and patted Julie's arm. "I'm very sorry that your son was so awful to you."

"My ex-husband has a way of making anyone believe any lie he wants, I'm afraid." Julie let out a deep sigh. "Right now, my son is in London and I'm here at this awful ski resort. We're worlds apart, the two of us. Maybe, for now…as much as it hurts me to admit it…that's best. My son, I fear, is going to learn the hard way that my ex-husband isn't a white knight. Until then, there is nothing I can do except pray and wait, love."

"Pray and wait…that's all anyone can really do," Bethany whispered. "I've been praying ever since we left the hunting lodge."

"Me too," Julie admitted. She looked toward the staircase.

Nothing but cold shadows stood at the bottom of the staircase. "I have to admit that right now I'm very scared and very confused. I keep wondering who you spoke to on the telephone."

"Me too," Bethany admitted in a miserable voice. "If I didn't speak to Shelia Vermont, who did I speak with, Julie? And why would the person I spoke with try to lure me to this ski lodge? It doesn't make any sense." Bethany shook her head. "Why did that old man have to leave that silly book in my coffee shop?"

"I don't—" Julie began to answer but nearly jumped out of her skin when Claude fired off a single rifle shot.

"Let's go!" Bethany yelled. She grabbed Julie's hand and took off running for the dining room expecting more rifle shots to explode. Bethany burst into a dark dining room filled with old tables that were covered with dusty sheets. "Claude...Samantha?" she cried out, struggling to see through a heavy dark fog.

"In the kitchen!" Claude's voice thundered into the dining room through an open kitchen door on a far back wall.

Bethany and Julie carefully followed Claude's voice and managed to find an open door that led into a dark, cold kitchen soaked with cobwebs and rusted appliances. Bethany spotted a beam of light focused on what appeared to be an old walk-in freezer. She hurried into the kitchen, stepping on a creaky hardwood floor, and ran to Claude and Samantha with Julie at her side. "What is it—"

"Take a look," Claude told Bethany and Julie in a voice that was more shaky than calm. He nodded toward the walk-in freezer. The door to the freezer was standing open. "Sam, stand back, but keep the light on the freezer floor."

Samantha did as her husband told her. She stepped back on wobbly legs and aimed the flashlight she was holding down at a dead body. Bethany and Julie made their way past Claude and looked into the freezer. "Oh my..." Julie cried out as soon as her eyes spotted a dead woman lying on the freezer floor. She threw her hands over her mouth and swung around to face Claude.

Claude quickly pulled Julie close to him. "It's going to be all right, you hear me?" he said, struggling to comfort Julie. "Me and Sam…we're gonna take care of you."

Bethany stared at the dead woman lying on the freezer floor with wide, terrified eyes. *All right…stay calm…don't panic. Think. Remain functional…just like one of the characters in your book…don't panic…remain calm…think…remain functional.* Bethany forced her eyes to remain on the dead woman. The poor woman was lying facedown. Was the woman Shelia Vermont? Bethany didn't know. All Bethany did know was that a very ugly and deadly kitchen knife was plunged in between the dead woman's shoulder blades. "Is this woman Shelia Vermont?" Bethany asked.

"Shelia has black hair…this woman…her hair is blonde…," Samantha struggled to answer Bethany. Tough or not, the sight of a dead woman was enough to cripple anyone.

"That woman ain't Shelia," Claude confirmed, fighting to regain his composure. "I can tell." Claude let go of Julie. He stepped next to Bethany and forced his eyes to look down at the dead woman lying in the freezer. "I ain't never seen that woman before. We best…find a blanket and cover her body."

Bethany lifted her eyes off the dead woman lying in the freezer and looked at Claude. "Claude…we're in serious trouble," she stated in a voice that caused everyone to stand very still and very silent.

"Yes, you are," a hideous voice whispered and then slithered back into the front room and vanished upstairs on silent legs. "You're all going to die…one by one."

chapter four

R*un? Scream? Hide? Panic? What should we do?* Bethany felt her heart pounding hard in her chest as her frantic mind tried to comprehend the entirety of the situation. Julie, Samantha, and Claude were no better off. Samantha was on the verge of insisting everyone return to the snowcat—which wasn't such a bad idea; at least in Bethany's eyes. *We're alone on this mountain. There are no cops to call, no one to depend on…if we're going to survive…we're going to have to survive on our own.* Bethany felt as if she had suddenly become trapped in a real-life horror movie…some B-rated horror movie titled *Murder at the Ski Resort* or *Deadly Edge.* Only the situation she and her friends were trapped in was filled with authentic horror instead of cheesy screams. "All right, let's get back to the front room…we'll cancel searching the lodge for now."

Claude slammed shut the door to the walk-in freezer. "I agree with you, Bethany."

"We need to lock ourselves in the cat," Samantha insisted. "We have blankets, Claude. We can risk the cold.

"We'll freeze to death before first light, Sam, and you know it. It's cold enough outside to freeze a man's shadow in place." Claude shook his head. "We best get back to the front room. Come on." Claude took his wife's hand. "It'll be all right."

Samantha wasn't so sure her husband was speaking the truth. Instead of debating the issue, she followed Claude back to the front room. Bethany and Julie followed with their eyes on alert and their ears peeled. *The dead woman was wearing a heavy blue sweater…no winter coat. She wasn't wearing a winter hat…had on a pair of heavy brown pants…black snow boots. It seems clear to me that she was dressed to remain indoors and that the lodge was warm at the time of her death. There's a lot of questions. Who is the woman? Why was she killed? It's clear that the woman was attacked.* Bethany fought with a mountain of questions as she hurried back to the front room of the lodge. The fire was still standing strong in the stone fireplace, untouched and left alone. "Claude, what does Shelia Vermont look like?"

"She's a black-haired woman…about your age…always reminded me of that actress who played the mom on the television show *Growing Pains*. I remember that television show because my daughter used to always make me watch it with her while she was growing up." Claude eyed the fireplace. "For thirty minutes, me and my daughter just sat back and enjoyed a silly old television show…those were the good days."

"Yes, they were," Samantha agreed, staring at the fireplace with deeply worried eyes.

Samantha doesn't believe anyone is going to leave the ski resort alive. I can read her eyes. The poor dear…she's trying to appear so brave, but on the inside, she's terrified. "Claude, you told me and Julie that you took Shelia's husband down the mountain. Was there anyone else at the ski resort when you picked up Shelia's husband…besides her dad?"

"Nobody that I saw," Claude answered Bethany. Claude had to admit that he was feeling extremely vulnerable and overly exposed to an unseen enemy. "I left Shelia and her old man here at the ski resort and drove her husband back down the mountain. Sam was with me." Claude shook his head. "I can't tell you the exact day...seems like it was a few weeks ago...give or take a couple of days, I guess. Sometimes it's easy to lose tracks. The days seem to fade into each other...."

"Yes, that's true." Samantha nodded. "Sometimes I think it's Monday and it'll almost be time for the Holy Sabbath. Time isn't tamed in the Alaskan wilderness." Samantha turned to look at Bethany. "Why are you asking these questions, honey?"

Bethany scanned the front room. Was a killer...or killers... lurking about in the darkness? Bethany didn't know. "Shelia Vermont and her dad are missing. You found the body of a dead woman that isn't Shelia Vermont. How did the dead woman get to the ski resort?" Bethany quickly folded her arms together as she continued to look around. "The dead woman was dressed in a way that tells me the lodge was warm at the time of her death. She was also dressed in a way that appeared to be comfortable. I also noticed that the sides of the dead woman's hair were braided...very stylish, actually."

"Love, are you suggesting the poor woman lying in that awful freezer was some sort of guest?" Julie asked.

"No...not necessarily a guest...but...an invited visitor." *But who?* Bethany wondered. *And where are Shelia Vermont and her dad? Where is the old man who visited my coffee shop?* "I checked the dead woman's pants pockets. Nothing." Bethany nodded toward the wooden staircase. "I think we might need to check the upstairs guest rooms."

"I was afraid you were going to say that." Julie gulped. "Bethany...maybe we should stay downstairs in the open. There's four of us...no one should be able to sneak up on us and attack."

Bethany knew Julie was right. *Yes. Julie is right. I don't need to go traipsing off upstairs to play Nancy Drew. If a killer is hiding upstairs, I don't want to make myself an easy target. The only problem is, Shelia Vermont and her dad are missing. Could one of them be the killer? Possibly. But why? Why would Shelia Vermont or her dad leave the ski resort dark and cold with a dead body lying in a freezer knowing that Julie and I were on our way? Surely Shelia Vermont and her dad would know that Claude would be driving Julie and me up the mountain in his snowcat. None of this makes any sense. I wish Sarah was here. Sarah is so smart and brave. She's a famous homicide detective. Me...I'm just a beaten-down widow who can barely put one thought in front of the other.* "I guess you're right, Julie."

"Maybe she is right, but we need answers," Claude demanded. "Bethany, if we make it off this mountain alive, we're going to have to report the killing to the cops. I don't want to be suspected of killing the woman we saw. I want to go to the cops with at least a handful of possible answers." Claude shook his head. "The cops up in these parts are about as smart as a chicken trying to make friends with a hungry fox. Cops just don't have no interest in the truth and turn hostile toward anyone who causes them to get off their butts and do their job."

"I'm afraid Claude is right," Samantha supported her husband. "It would be best to have some answers to take to the cops...well, if you can call three men who pretend to be the law cops. In the county our hunting lodge sits in, it's really...well, every man for himself."

"The three badges who claim to be the law in our county aren't worth snot," Claude scowled. "Be that as it may, I'd rather have some answers in my belt to give them in order to protect us, Sam. Can you agree with that?"

"I can." Samantha nodded in sorrow rather than confidence. "Claude, I would much rather go back to the cat and wait until morning and then try to walk down the mountain. I would much rather risk freezing to death rather than being killed. But I know you're not going to agree."

"A woman is dead, Sam. I can't walk away. If we hadn't found the woman…then maybe…." Claude shook his head again. "Wiley is a hard man, Sam. If I show up empty-handed, he'll try to hammer me down to the ground. Even if that wasn't so…I can't walk away from a dead woman. Wouldn't be right." Claude eyed the front room with careful eyes. "I don't know who the dead woman is. Was she a decent sort or a bad seed? I don't know, Sam. All I know is that I'm a man, and a man has a job to do."

"And that's why I love you, Claude." Samantha reached out and took her husband's left hand. "My heart is rattled a little, that's all. I keep imagining you and me ending up in that dark freezer. I know you and me ain't important to this world…invisible, really. Our daughter loves us…" Samantha's voice broke some.

Claude squeezed his wife's hand. "Sam, we're going to get off this mountain. You'll see," he promised. "I aim fast and shoot straight."

"I know…" Samantha tried to put on a brave face. "I guess we better get upstairs."

"Guess we should. But this time we go as a team." Claude nodded at Bethany and Julie. "Wherever Sam and I go, you two go. Is that clear?"

"Clear," Bethany promised.

"Clear," Julie added in a grateful voice. She hurried over to Claude and hugged his free arm. "You're quite great, you know. Samantha is blessed to have you as her husband."

"I agree," Bethany told Claude. "If you weren't here, I wouldn't know what to do."

"Aw…just trying to do what a man is born to do," Claude said, blushing a little. He wasn't used to two women giving him special attention. Bethany and Julie were quickly wearing on Claude's heart—becoming like two daughters to him. "Well, let's go have a look around upstairs."

"I guess we should." Samantha focused on the shadowy

staircase as cold white moisture left her mouth. The fire sitting in the fireplace was losing a battle against the cold. The front room felt like a cold, icy morgue.

Bethany checked the gun she was holding with a gloved hand. The gun was secure and ready for action. "Aim fast and shoot straight," Claude told her in a strong, firm tone.

"I will." Bethany raised her eyes and looked at Claude. Claude was wearing a concerned expression that sent a deep worry soaring into Bethany's heart. *He doesn't believe we're going to leave the ski resort alive, either. His eyes are hiding his true thoughts.* Bethany continued to stare into Claude's eyes. *The snowcat has no gas. A woman is dead. A killer...or multiple killers...are hiding in the storm somewhere. Shelia Vermont and her dad are missing. Yes. Claude thinks we're not going to see the morning light arrive...and he may be right. But for now, all we can do is seek answers...who knows? Maybe seeking some answers might help us stay alive? It can't hurt.*

Bethany checked the gun she was holding one more time and then began walking over toward the staircase. Julie followed. Claude and Samantha took up the rear. Slowly and carefully, Bethany began climbing up the creaky wooden staircase on legs that felt scared and weak. *I endured years of being married to an abusive man. I survived that awful marriage all alone...I can do this...because this time I'm not alone. I have Julie, Samantha, and Claude. And Julie is right...Claude may be a fussy old fart, but he's great. I can depend on him. So be brave...as the Lord told Joshua...be strong and of good courage.*

One step followed another step. Bethany carefully climbed upward into a dark abyss. Samantha flicked on the flashlight she was holding and tossed some light into Bethany's path. The weak light flowing from the flashlight pushed back the cold darkness only a few measly inches. If a killer was lurking in the darkness on the second level and preparing to attack... Bethany couldn't see. "Aim fast and shoot straight," she whispered as her legs reached the top floor.

Claude watched Bethany swing to her right and then to her left, examining both sides of a long, dark hallway. He hurried Julie and Samantha up onto the landing and then focused on the right side of the hallway. "Sam, throw the light down that way," he ordered. Samantha did as her husband asked. She used the flashlight to examine the right side of a dark hallway. The light only gave life to a line of closed doors. "Give light to the other side of the hallway, Sam." Samantha turned and began dousing the left side of the hallway with as much light as possible. Nothing but closed doors appeared. Claude narrowed his eyes. "All right, we'll start with the left side of the hallway and work our way down to the apartment door. Bethany, you take the lead. Sam and me will cover the rear. Julie, you stay in the middle of us."

Bethany drew in a deep breath and carefully walked down the left portion of the hallway until she reached room number 1. The door was firmly closed. *Well, there's no use in delaying the inevitable.* Bethany reached out her left hand and tried a rusted doorknob. To her dismay rather than relief, the doorknob offered no resistance.

"Easy…," Claude threw out in a loud whisper.

Bethany felt her heart nearly leap out of her chest as she slowly pushed the door open. The door creaked and moaned in a loud cry. If a killer was hiding in the dark room beyond the door…well, the creaking door was a dead giveaway that someone was entering the room. *Silly old door.* Bethany bit down on her lower lip and forced herself to stick her head through the doorway while holding the gun Claude had given her at the ready position. "Samantha…I need light."

Samantha nodded, dashed past Julie, and had the flashlight she was holding perched over Bethany's shoulder in no time. Weak, cold light splashed onto a room that held a run-down bed, a battered writing desk, and a sitting chair that was covered over with a white sheet. No other furnishings stood in the room that Bethany could see. *All I see is a bed…a writing desk…a chair covered over with a sheet…a bare wooden floor…log walls…a closed closet door and a bare window.* "I don't see anyone, Claude."

Claude hurried to the doorway. He threw his eyes into the room, looked around the best he could, and then glanced back up the hallway. "Julie, you stand right here in this doorway while me and Bethany check the closet."

"All right." Julie perched herself in the doorway as Claude stepped into the dark room with Bethany and Samantha. She watched as the trio cautiously checked an empty closet filled with cold cobwebs. "I guess—" Julie began to speak into the room but stopped when she heard a door slowly start to creak open. Someone was in one of the rooms! The killer? Who else could it be?

"Someone is coming out of one of the rooms!" Julie's voice pierced the dark air like a frantic child screaming for her parents while watching a hideous closet door containing a terrifying monster start to open.

Claude's old soldier instincts jumped into action. He charged out into the hallway like a brave combat veteran preparing to go toe-to-toe with a dangerous enemy. To his shock, Bethany trailed him without the slightest hesitation. Claude heard a door opening somewhere down the hallway. "Stay here!" he yelled at Julie. "Sam, stay with her…Bethany, you're with me! Let's move!"

Bethany felt a rush of adrenaline pound her heart. She didn't have time to think or create a plan. Reaction based off mere survival instinct kicked in. She ran after Claude like an infantry soldier following a brave combat officer into battle. Claude had his hunting rifle stationed out in front of his body like a man carrying a spear. The old man ran down the hallway prepared to either kill or be killed. *I hear a door opening…a few doors down…getting closer…Claude is in the lead…he'll attack first…if something happens to him, it's up to me…dear Lord, give me courage….*

Claude ran past the stairwell and moved farther down the right side of the hallway. A dark shadow was stepping out of one of the closed doors. "You there…hands in the air…I'll shoot you down where you stand!" Claude hollered in a tone that meant serious business.

"Don't shoot…please!" a woman cried out in a voice that appeared to be harmed and consumed with pain. "Please… help…me…."

"Shelia?" Claude asked, stammering.

"Claude…is…that you?" Shelia Vermont managed to ask and then dropped down onto her knees. "Claude…help me…please…"

"Sam!" Claude hollered down the hallway. "Get up here! Bring Julie!" Claude hurried to the shadowy figure in the hall. Bethany watched as the man bent down without relaxing his rifle. "Shelia…what happened? Who is in the lodge? Talk to me."

"I…was attacked…my dad…" Shelia struggled to answer Claude.

Samantha ran down the hallway with Julie in tow. She bypassed Bethany and moved to Claude. Bethany watched as Samantha bent low and aimed the flashlight she was holding into a face that appeared to be weak and fragile. "Shelia… thank the Lord you're still alive. We found a dead woman in the kitchen freezer. Honey…what happened? Please, talk to us."

Bethany quickly soaked in every feature of Shelia Vermont's face. The woman did indeed have black hair— short, curly, black hair. A face that was pretty—not beautiful, but simply pretty—glowed in the weak light the flashlight was putting out. *She looks like a 1970s spokeswoman for some ski lodge ad.* Bethany scanned the outfit Shelia was wearing. *Looks like she's wearing a green sweater...a tan pair of slacks...brown boots.* A worried feeling attacked Bethany's mind. She bit down on her lip, made a quick decision, and then hurried to Shelia. Without saying a word, she bent down and took the woman's right hand with her left hand. "It'll be all right... take a minute and gather your thoughts."

No one knew that Bethany was deliberately feeling Shelia's hand. *Ice cold...I thought maybe her hands might be warm.* Bethany glanced into Shelia's face. Being up close and personal allowed her a better view. Authentic, paralyzing fear dripped from Shelia's eyes like sharp razors. *This woman is scared to death...and her face is red from being so cold. I guess my assumption was wrong.* "Who are you?" Shelia asked Bethany in a shaky voice.

"Don't you know?" Claude asked. Shelia shook her head no. "Shelia, that's Bethany Lights and Julie Walsh...you invited them to the ski lodge, or so they claim. We're starting to think maybe someone else invited them...Why, we don't know."

"I...don't know who these women are." Shelia pulled her hand away from Bethany. "Claude...I don't know what you're talking about."

"It's all right," Bethany struggled to speak in a soothing voice. "I think my friend and I might have been lured to this ski resort. Why, we don't know." Bethany looked deeply into Shelia's eyes. *This poor woman is terrified. I better back off and give her some space.*

Shelia watched as Bethany stood up and backed up to her friend. "Honey," Samantha said, taking Shelia's bare hands with a gloved hand, "what happened? Who is the dead woman we found? Where is your old man?"

"Dad...is dead...," Shelia answered and then burst out into tears. "His body is in cabin number 4...I dragged his body into the cabin and ran back to the lodge...he's dead... someone shot him. I was nearly killed...I hid in this room...

up in an attic crawl space in the closet. I heard voices…I thought I heard Claude's voice." Shelia wiped at a stream of falling tears with trembling hands.

"Shelia, listen to me," Claude demanded, speaking in a firm but concerned tone. "Someone stole the reserve gas can I had hooked to the cat. The cat is on empty. I could drive the cat maybe three miles, if that. There's a storm raging outside…the winds are enough to slice a man in half…" Claude drew in a deep breath. "Listen to me…tell us who the dead woman is…tell us who tried to kill you."

Shelia lifted her left hand and shielded her eyes from the flashlight Samantha was aiming at her. "The woman is… was…my best friend. Her name…Mandy Pacemore…oh, Mandy…." Shelia bowed her head and cried even harder.

"Shelia, I never brought your friend up to this mountain. How did she get here?" Claude pressed. "Talk to me…a woman is dead, for crying out loud—"

"Two people are dead," Samantha corrected her husband.

Claude nodded. "Talk to me, Shelia. We need answers."

Bethany stepped closer to Julie, looked over her shoulder at a dark hallway, and then bit down on her lip. Julie glanced over into her friend's face with concerned eyes. "What is it?" she whispered.

"I'll tell you later," Bethany whispered back.

Shelia didn't hear Bethany and Julie whispering to each other. Her heart was beating so loud in her ears that she barely heard anything other than the raw fear eating away at a terrified heart. "He came out of nowhere…I was here yesterday with Dad. We were checking the roofs on the cabins to make sure they were holding from all the snow…and… then…someone shot Dad!" Shelia burst out into fresh tears. "Shot him in the back…."

Claude reached out and took Shelia's arm. "What about your friend? How did she get up on this mountain? Talk to me, woman!"

"Mandy hired a private helicopter to fly her in when the weather cleared…she's…a very wealthy woman…was a very wealthy woman. Divorced…wanted to get away from the world…." Shelia wiped at her tears with trembling hands. "Dad set everything up for her after he left the ski resort…I…there's more to the story…."

"What?" Samantha asked Shelia. "Honey, talk to us."

"It's all my fault that Mandy is dead!" Shelia cried out in agony. "I needed a financial supporter to help me prop up the ski resort. My husband and I…we were already on shaky ground. You…know that." Shelia refused to lift her head. She spoke like a broken rag doll. "He refused to give me any more money to dedicate to the ski resort…and then he left me high and dry. I knew that my husband was going to eventually leave me…he only traveled to the ski resort because he assumed a possible investment that could benefit him might be worth taking a look at. That's why I sent Dad away…to go talk to…Mandy. Mandy and I were closer than sisters…now she's dead and it's all my fault. She came here to help me… she was prepared to stay on at the ski resort for a long period of time…she didn't have a set day to leave…."

Bethany absorbed every word Shelia spoke. *I feel like Shelia Vermont is telling the truth. She could be lying, but I don't think she is. A woman knows.* "Shelia, who killed your dad and your friend? Do you know?"

Shelia shook her head no. "All I saw was a man wearing a black ski mask. He…when Mandy and I were in the downstairs area of the lodge…the man came out of nowhere and attacked us. I managed to escape…I heard Mandy screaming as I ran up the stairs…I…left her to die…I'll never forgive myself…."

"Did your friend arrive with anyone?" Bethany asked.

"No…I watched the helicopter arrive…drop Mandy off… and then fly away…that's the truth," Shelia cried. "That's the truth."

"I told you I thought I saw a helicopter, Claude…the day I was out getting firewood because your back was sore." Samantha looked around with uncertain eyes. A killer was on the loose. "What do we do, Claude?"

Claude lifted his left hand and rubbed the back of his neck. "I'm not entirely certain what to do," he confessed. "There's five of us now…and if Shelia is right…there is only one attacker. There's power in numbers…but if the attacker has a gun, he can pick us off one by one. We need to hunker down in a secured location."

"The apartment…there's a fire escape ladder attached to the bedroom window, Claude…I heard the apartment door open and close a few times while I was hiding in the attic crawl space," Shelia said through her tears. "I think that's how the man who killed Mandy has been getting in and out of the lodge." Shelia wiped at her tears. "Each room has an attic crawl space…but the attic has solid walls that separates each room…very difficult to get up into the attic crawl space. I've been up hiding since yesterday. I'm so tired…I haven't slept any…I have to use the bathroom really bad—"

Before Shelia could finish her words, a large explosion rocked the lodge. Claude jumped to his feet and grabbed his wife as a violent wave of power began shaking the upstairs hallway. Bethany threw her arms around Julie and hunkered down. Outside in the dark storm, a wall of rock exploded and crashed down…blocking the rock gap. Even if the snowcat that was sitting crippled out in the storm did have a spare can of gas…there was no way out of the ski resort except for a very dangerous back trail that was filled with deadly hazards that no man in his right mind would dare to challenge.

"Feels like an earthquake!" Julie exclaimed, holding on to Bethany for dear life.

Bethany didn't speak until the ground beneath her feet stopped shaking. "Claude?" she called out. "Talk to me."

"That was a dynamite blast. When I was a young man, I

worked in the mines…heard my share of dynamite blasts more times than I can count," Claude called back to Bethany. "If I had to take a guess, I would say someone just blew up the rock gap that leads into the ski resort…blocking us in for good."

"Which means we couldn't try to walk down the mountain even if we wanted to," Samantha moaned.

"A person would have to take that old back trail…but the back trail is like walking on a broken spine, Sam. I never walked it, but according to the map, the trail winds up and down and sideways…connecting to other trails. It would take a man a full week to walk down the trail…assuming he knew where he was going." Claude shook his head. "I'm just telling you what I saw on the map. Last time we were at this ski resort, Sam, I walked to the edge of the trail and had a look. Man would have to be crazy to try and navigate what I saw before my eyes."

"Shelia, do you know anything about the back trail?" Samantha asked in a desperate voice.

"No." Shelia raised a pair of shaky eyes. "I stay on the main trails that lead up to the top of the ski hills. I know how dangerous this mountain is and how easy it would be to get lost."

Bethany let go of Julie with hands that felt more uncertain by the second. *Why would someone lure me and Julie to this ski lodge…and then trap us? What is going on? Was it mere coincidence that Mr. Richtore left his book behind in my coffee shop? Was it mere coincidence that I confessed to the old man that I needed to get away from Snow Falls for a bit?* Bethany's mind struggled and fought to make sense of the dangerous situation she was trapped in—but failed. "Shelia," she said, becoming very stern and upset, "I spoke to a woman who pretended to be you. That woman invited me and my friend to this ski lodge, pretending that she needed two pairs of helping hands. I don't know who that woman was. Do you?"

"No, of course not." Shelia's eyes filled with desperation. "Claude, please, help me stand up. I feel very weak." Claude let go of his wife and used his left hand to help Shelia stand up. Shelia rose on a pair of unstable legs but managed to remain standing. "I don't know who the man that killed Mandy is...or my dad. I've been trapped in a stuffy attic crawl space since yesterday...but I've been listening."

"To what?" Bethany demanded.

"Footsteps," Shelia nearly snapped Bethany's head off. "My dad is dead...my best friend is dead...what do you think I've been doing? Sitting around polishing my nails?" Shelia let go of Claude's hand. "When your life is in danger, you learn to listen to every sound. I heard the man who killed Mandy enter the room I was in...I listened to his boots walk around the room. I heard him open the closet door. I...just knew that awful man was going to find me and...kill me... but he left the room." Shelia dropped her shoulders. "One pair of footsteps...no more...one man...one killer...that's all I've been hearing since yesterday...since Mandy was killed...."

"Two people are dead. Claude thinks that the entrance way into this cursed ski resort was just blown to pieces. Now what? There's no way possible to communicate with the outside world. The snowcat doesn't have any gas. A killer is on the loose. Julie and I were lured to this ski resort for some unknown reason...nothing makes sense." Bethany felt like screaming. *No. That's not the answer. If Sarah were here, she would remain calm and thoughtful...functional. If I'm going to make it out of this ski resort alive with Julie, Samantha, and Claude...and Shelia Vermont, it appears...I'm going to have to remain calm and take control of this situation. If there's one thing I've learned during my years, it's that there's always a reason behind insanity.* "The kitchen would be the ideal spot to stay in," she said. "There are only two doors, and the kitchen has a wood-burning stove that we can use for heat." *At least that's a start…maybe. Who knows what kind of a killer we're dealing with?*

Outside in the storm, a vicious killer grinned as he stared at a mountain of fallen rock that was quickly turning into a mountain of deep snow. "No one leaves the ski resort alive," he hissed and then began working his way back toward the ski lodge. "No one."

chapter five

Claude managed to start a fire in an old, rusted wood-burning stove that belonged in the house of Laura Ingalls Wilder. As Claude worked on the fire, Shelia fussed with a rustic lantern that eventually came to life. Cold light began glowing from the lantern, bringing a little life to the kitchen Bethany had suggested everyone hunker down in. Remaining in the front room, she knew, would have been foolish. *We need four strong walls and as few entrances and exits as possible. We don't need to make it easy for the killer to get at us.* "We barricaded the dining room door. The door leading into the kitchen is barricaded. The only way in and out of this kitchen now is through that back door." Bethany pointed to a solid wood door stationed on a back wall that was covered with stone instead of log. "The kitchen doesn't have any windows…which is a blessing—"

"The storms on this mountain are too strong," Shelia cut in, standing close to the wood-burning stove with Samantha and Julie. Bethany noticed that Shelia was becoming very irritable. "The original owner had many windows covered over with solid walls. I've boarded up all the windows in the cabins."

Bethany simply nodded. "We're secure in the kitchen. The

killer will have to fight his way in to get at us...or use dynamite to blow us out of here." The thought of being blown into the storm did not appeal to anyone—neither did standing in a large room as open targets. For the time being, everyone agreed that the kitchen was the best option. Now that Claude had some answers, he didn't mind digging in and waiting for morning to arrive.

"Maybe now we can try and figure out who you talked to, Bethany?" Julie suggested in a voice that she hoped sounded calm. Standing in the kitchen wasn't very horrible. Standing close to a walk-in freezer that was holding a dead body was a completely different story. Americans were strange and dangerous creatures that scared Julie.

Bethany wanted to ease close to the wood-burning stove, but for the time being, Samantha, Julie, and Shelia were occupying every possible space around the stove as Claude continued to build a strong fire with wood he brought to the kitchen from the front room. "The wood we all carried into this kitchen won't last forever," Claude cautioned. "We should have just enough wood to run us to first light, then we're either going to have to start breaking this kitchen apart or make another run."

Bethany eyed a round wooden table and decided to sit down. Her legs ached and cried from the cold. *I'm so tired I can barely think straight. I'm also hungry and thirsty. My entire body aches. I've never been so cold in all of my life. Oh, the joy of living in Alaska!* A fierce bitterness seeped from Bethany's exhausted heart. *First, I had to suffer through years of an abusive marriage, and now I'm going to either freeze to death or be killed by some crazy...snowman. Life is grand.*

"Bethany?" Julie asked in a careful voice. "What are you thinking?" Julie knew her friend well enough to know when something was the matter.

"Oh...I suppose I'm sitting here feeling sorry for myself," Bethany confessed to Julie and then sighed. "I wish we were back home in Snow Falls, sitting in a nice, safe, warm living room playing Scrabble and complaining about how we're probably never going to meet two good men and get married someday."

"I wish we were home too, love," Julie said in a voice that was filled with desperate exhaustion. "I had hoped this holiday would allow me to have the time I would need to work out all of my pain and frustrations. I truly wanted to take this holiday in order to travel far away from the world and…be close to God rather than the world."

Samantha reached over and patted Julie's hand. "Honey, God isn't far away…don't matter if we live or die, God isn't far away."

"That's right." Claude stood up and closed the iron door attached to the wood-burning stove. He brushed off the gloves he was wearing onto his coat, looked around the kitchen, and snatched his rifle. "When my old man was dying…oh, he was ninety-four…he never stopped smiling, even though he had a bad cancer."

"I remember," Samantha cut in. "I remember that you asked your old man why he was smiling all the time, especially since he refused to be given any morphine for his pain."

"Know what my old man told me?" Claude asked Bethany, Julie, and Shelia.

"What?" Julie asked.

A gentle smile touched Claude's face, shocking everyone —including Samantha; it wasn't often that Claude smiled. "My old man told me he was smiling because he was constantly seeing Jesus standing just outside of a beautiful city that glowed like bright gold." Claude nodded. "My old man wasn't much in the imagination department…he was a man who saw black and white. What he told me about Jesus and Heaven as he lay dying…well…let's just say that when he took his last breath, I envied him."

"It was a very peaceful death," Samantha agreed as heat from the wood-burning stove began to slowly fight back a cruel cold mouth that was devouring the kitchen. "I don't have no fear of dying myself...when it's my time, Claude. I don't want to die at the hands of some lunatic. I always imagined myself dying the same way your old man did...the same way your mother died...peacefully...lying in a warm bed, staring into the face of our Lord and Savior Jesus Christ."

Bethany locked her eyes on the lantern that was sitting on the wooden table she was sitting beside. "There has to be a logical explanation for all of this," she insisted. "There has to be some sort of...sinister...plan that was created. I know my words might sound insane, but I can't get around the fact that Julie and I were lured to this ski resort for a reason."

"We have nothing but time. Speak your thoughts." Claude eyed the back door and then joined Bethany at the kitchen table and sat down. "My back is hurting something fierce. Won't hurt for me to rest for a bit and let my ears get some exercise."

"Bethany, what are you thinking?" Julie asked.

"Well...this might sound crazy...but I think...." Bethany winced some. "I think maybe Shelia's dad might not be dead."

"What?" Shelia gasped. "Are you insane? I saw my dad get shot right before my eyes!"

"Yes, that's what you told us." Bethany prepared to drop a few depth charges into Shelia's heart. *My mind keeps going back to the old man who visited my coffee shop. He was such a talkative old man...very nice...asked me all kinds of questions about myself...told me all about himself...and then he left his book behind. Why? I'm starting to wonder if the old man...Mr. Richtore...left his book behind because I told him I always had a curious mind and I wanted to know all about the history of Alaska. But goodness, I was simply making conversation with an old man. I was simply being*

nice. But could it be that the old man was playing me for a fool?
"Shelia, Mr. Richtore, your dad, how old was he?"

"Seventy-eight. Why?" Shelia asked.

"Where did Mr. Richtore live?" Bethany pressed.

"Rhode Island. Why are you asking me these questions?" Shelia demanded.

"What did Mr. Richtore do for a living?" Bethany hated herself for attacking Shelia, but she needed answers.

Shelia stared at Bethany with eyes that turned very sour. "Real estate," she answered in a bitter tone. "My dad helped me purchase this ski lodge. And before you ask...no, my husband didn't pitch in one penny. I used my inheritance. My husband came along, as I already pointed out, because he thought this ski lodge might be a solid investment that could earn him some money. We...were already on the verge of divorce. I wasn't very thrilled that my husband insisted on seeing the ski resort. Divorce can be very messy, and I was afraid he might try and steal the ski resort from me. I was more than happy when my husband threw up his hands and left."

"At the same time your dad showed up," Bethany pointed out.

"That's not a coincidence. Neil...that's the skunk I'm married to...told my dad when he would be leaving, regardless if he saw my ski resort as a gold mine or not. My husband does have a career. He owns a chain of restaurants in New Hampshire that he eventually had to return to."

Bethany slowly folded her arms in order to keep warm rather than to relax. "Shelia, where did your friend Mandy live?"

Shelia's eyes locked on a closed freezer door. "Shelia lived in Arizona...Phoenix. She moved to Arizona after her husband accepted a position there...head of neurology, if I remember correct. Mandy's husband was a doctor...but a real jerk. Arrogant, selfish, hateful…Mandy endured a lot of bad years."

Sounds like Mandy and I had a lot in common. Bethany glanced toward the walk-in freezer. "Shelia, my friend Sarah helped me locate a phone number to this ski resort. We found the number on a website—"

"A website?" Shelia threw her eyes back at Bethany in disbelief. "That's impossible. I haven't created a website for the ski resort and neither has my husband. For goodness' sake, we've just recently been trying to fix the place up…well, I have. Neil hasn't been much help. He was more than happy to leave me on this mountain alone with Dad."

"This is all very strange," Julie had to admit. She walked away from the wood-burning stove and sat down next to Bethany. "I think…maybe…someone could be wanting this ski resort other than Shelia," she stated.

Bethany considered Julie's words. *Could it be that someone does want this ski resort for some reason? Could it be that Julie and I were lured here to…to what? Be framed for murder? The idea of being framed for murder suddenly jumped off the page at Bethany. Maybe someone wants Shelia dead? Maybe that someone might be her husband?* Bethany felt a few locked gears trapped in her mind start to give. Curious questions began flowing out of a back dusty room that was home to a thoughtful writer who was currently suffering from writer's block. *Surely the killer would have torn apart this lodge to find Shelia…yet, he left Shelia untouched…alive…why? Did Shelia truly find a secure hiding spot or did the killer simply leave her alive? It doesn't make sense that the killer would have overlooked a hiding location that seemed… well, obvious. If I was a killer, I would have checked every crook and cranny in this lodge. Yet, the killer left Shelia untouched—but Shelia's friend is dead. Why?*

"Speak your mind," Claude ordered Bethany. "I can read your eyes. Your hamster is running."

Bethany walked her eyes upward and looked toward Shelia. "Shelia, what made you want to buy this ski lodge?"

"That's personal," Shelia snapped at Bethany before she could catch her tongue. "I mean, my reasons are personal."

"I understand that," Bethany assured Shelia, "but at this point, I think it's important you tell everyone why you wanted to buy a remote Alaskan ski lodge that does seem to be without...hope."

"I wondered that myself," Samantha told Shelia.

"Same here," Claude added as he laid his hunting rifle across his lap.

"It does seem curious," Julie told Shelia. "Love, maybe you should, as you Americans say, spill the beans?"

Shelia began to feel like a trapped animal. However, Mandy was dead...her dad was dead, or so it seemed, and a deadly killer was on the loose. Maybe it was time to confess the truth—or maybe it was time to play very smart. "Do you really want to know the truth?" she asked, pretending to allow defeat to crash down onto her heart like a violent wave.

"Please," Bethany pressed.

"All right, then, this is the truth." Shelia walked over to the back door and checked a strong deadbolt lock. "My husband has a mistress. Who? I don't know. nor do I care." Shelia kept her back turned as she spoke. "I became sick of the world I was forced to...exist in...a world filled with cruelty, hate, crime, corruption...endless traffic jams. No. I needed a change."

"Alaska?" Julie asked.

"Not at first, no," Shelia confessed. "My dad had retired and sold his real estate business by the time I found out my husband was being...unfaithful. I went to my dad and confessed everything. I told him that I wanted...no, that I desperately needed...to escape the world. My dad...he was the one who told me about this ski resort. I had my sights set on a small island in the South Pacific—a far cry from Alaska, I know."

"Why did Mr. Richtore suggest a run-down, deserted ski resort?" Bethany asked.

Shelia slowly turned to face everyone. "Gold," she answered in a simple voice. "My dad, rest his sweet soul, spent all of his spare time searching for lost treasures. I can't begin to tell you how many times he dived under the oceans searching for sunken ships." Shelia dropped her shoulders. "I have my dad's blood in me. When he told me about this ski resort...about how the ski resort holds a legend about lost gold...well, what did I have to lose? Even if we didn't find any missing gold, the idea of owning a ski resort in Alaska appealed to me. So...here I am."

"That's why Mr. Richtore seemed so excited," Bethany said in a quick voice, speaking more to herself than to anyone else. "And maybe that's why your husband decided to travel to this mountain and have a look at the ski resort?" she finished, turning her words directly at Shelia.

"You're a very smart woman. What do you want? A lollipop?" Shelia asked.

"No, I want answers...and I'm starting to think maybe the answers I need are drifting into my mind through a thick fog." Bethany studied Shelia's face with smart eyes. "Shelia —" she began to speak but stopped when a hard blast of wind struck the back door. Bethany waited a few seconds and began to continue but then stopped. Without understanding how or why she knew...Bethany sensed that someone was standing just outside the back door in the storm...waiting to strike.

Neil Vermont tucked his head down against a powerful gust of wind that sliced into his body. "They're not going anywhere in this storm. I need to warm up." Neil glared at a closed back door with deadly eyes and then faded back through deep snow and began working his way toward a dark cabin. The wind was causing dangerous snowdrifts to pile up against the lodge and the line of cabins that complimented the lodge; cabins designed to house rich and spoiled people who demanded stronger privacy. Working his way through the storm, the deep snow, and deadly winds was extremely difficult. Neil felt frozen to the core. By the time he reached number 4, the killer felt as if his entire body was nothing more than an iceberg.

"Shut the door!" John Richtore snapped at Neil. "You'll let the heat out!"

"All right...all right." Neil stepped into a warm front room and hurried to close a thick wooden door. The windows to the room were boarded up. No one from the outside could see that four lanterns were sitting in the room along with a kerosene heater.

"I heard the explosion. Good."

Neil ripped a black mask off his face, revealing a fat, ugly —hateful—mask that stood in stark contrast to Shelia's pretty facial features. "I nearly blew myself up! The fuse needed to be longer!" Neil glared at a scrawny old man that reminded him of Alistair Sim from the movie *A Christmas Carol*. John was sitting on a dusty brown chair like a deadly spider slowly spinning a vicious web in his mind.

"You're alive, aren't you?" John asked.

"Barely." John moved toward a gray kerosene heater that was sitting in the middle of a medium-sized room coated with dust, cold, and time. Two doors sat at the far end of the room. One door opened up to a small bedroom and the second door offered a path into a dark bathroom. No kitchen was attached to the cabin. All food had to be acquired at the lodge. "Everyone moved into the kitchen."

"Oh?" John folded his hands over a heavy gray coat.

"They're not going anywhere."

"Are you sure of that?" John asked in a venomous voice.

"The snowcat that Claude Stewart owns has no gas. I stole the reserve gas can. I blew up the only entrance to the ski resort. I doubt they're going to risk taking the back trail in this storm." Neil snatched off a pair of heavy black gloves and began warming his hands. "No one is moving until morning. I need to warm up."

John glared at Neil with sour eyes. He despised his daughter's so-called husband. The man looked like a fat blimp wearing a black curtain. Only a set of messy red hair gave the soulless tick color. "We need a heavy body count." John narrowed his eyes. "Shelia should be dead by now."

"I couldn't find her—"

"Maybe you didn't want to find my daughter?" John snapped.

"You're a worthless rat, John." Neil shook his head. "For a man to turn on his own daughter—"

"You killed Mandy—"

"I know who I killed!" Neil snapped at John in a tone that caused the old man to unfold his hands and lift a gun that was laying in his lap. "Put the gun down. You're nothing without me and you know it, so calm down. I'll get to Shelia in time."

"Perhaps…" John studied Neil's angry face with clever eyes. "Mandy was going to speak the truth to Shelia. She was going to tell Shelia that you two were…in love, dare I say. Now all you have to do is kill Julie Walsh and the Stewarts… and let Ms. Bethany Lights take a very hard fall."

"I still don't know why you lured those two women up here," Neil demanded.

A hideous grin touched John's skeletal face. "When I found out that Bethany Lights was an author and that she wrote a murder mystery book…words from the woman's own mouth, by the way…I decided to use her to place her on a very complicated chess board in order to trap the King. Call it…mere coincidence if you will, but when I went to visit your darling…wolf…I saw her reading the very same book Ms. Bethany Lights brought to life. I didn't think much of the book until I met Ms. Lights in Snow Falls. Even then I wasn't able to truly connect the dots—"

"Stop speaking in riddles," Neil complained.

John narrowed his eyes. "Very well," he hissed. "When Ms. Lights located the website Mandy created for the ski resort, a website that wasn't supposed to have been live, by the way, I decided to act. You see, the book Ms. Lights wrote demonstrates, if you will, the perfect murder. Your darling wolf, Neil, was using the woman's book as a blueprint to kill you. But I'm getting ahead of myself." John leaned back in his chair. "When Ms. Lights called the number on the website Mandy created, I was somewhat shocked. Mandy did a splendid job pretending to be Shelia…or so she claimed. What else could she do? Mandy admitted to me that she panicked when Bethany called her. The brain-dead woman even went so far as to admit that she clumsily confessed that help was needed at the ski resort…oh, how Mandy always used to babble on and on—"

"Get to the point!" Neil demanded. "I know how Mandy used to babble!"

John folded his hands together. "Why did Bethany Lights attempt to contact Shelia? The woman claimed that she made contact to try and locate me in order to return a book I accidentally left behind…at my age, sometimes you do forget."

"I don't—"

"The website Mandy created isn't a website that can be easily located," John pushed through Neil's broken words. "I began to wonder who Ms. Bethany Lights truly was. Of course, I was at the hunting lodge and had very little time to truly get my thoughts together, but I decided that I couldn't leave any loose ends. I ordered Mandy to contact Ms. Lights and ask her to travel to the ski resort. I was unaware that Ms. Lights was going to bring a friend. Oh well…what is one more body?"

"You're not making any sense!" Neil was ready to kill John with his bare hands.

"The gold, you incompetent moron!" John snapped. "Is Ms. Lights aware of the gold…somehow? Did the woman connect the dots using the book I left behind? I don't know. Mandy was reading the woman's book. In her secret diary, I read her own words…she was reading the book as a murder blueprint! I have the diary. I can connect Mandy to Ms. Lights…I can wrap it all up! I can make it appear that Ms. Lights was manipulating a very fragile woman to kill off my daughter in order to take control of the ski resort and in return, Ms. Lights would help her kill you. But you managed to stay alive…save my life…and Ms. Lights goes off to prison for life."

"You're insane." Neil shook his head. "John, you're—"

"Shelia knows where the gold is. She is planning to take the gold from me…oh, that woman is a skilled liar. She can deceive anyone with her silver tongue." John felt anger flush through his snake-like eyes. "You married a venomous spider, Neil."

"Don't remind me." Neil continued to warm his hands. He stood silent for a minute, struggling to piece together a very confusing scheme that seemed perfectly clear in the mind of a deadly old man. "What you're telling me is that you're worried Bethany Lights got wind of the gold and now you're trying to use the woman to take the fall for the murders—"

"You still have to perform," John finished for Neil. "Mandy was reading the same book Ms. Lights wrote. Coincidence? Maybe. Was it mere coincidence that I entered a coffee shop in Snow Falls that Ms. Lights owned? Maybe.

Maybe not. Did Mandy know Ms. Lights somehow? Was Mandy playing me for a fool? Was Mandy truly shocked when Ms. Lights made contact with her, expecting to be making contact with the ski lodge instead? Perhaps. Or maybe Mandy was playing me for a fool! After all, Mandy went only as far as Snow Falls before turning back...or so she claimed she was turning back toward Anchorage." John drew in a deep breath. "Or maybe it is all coincidence? Maybe my tired mind is polluted with paranoia? But at this juncture in the road, Neil, I'll depend on my paranoia to guide my thoughts."

"Whatever floats your boat, John."

"You brain-dead moron!" John exploded. "Do you know how close we are to finding the gold? Do you think I'm going to leave any loose strings flung about? Regardless of how Ms. Lights plays into this difficult act, in my mind, the woman is a threat. I'm going to use her to tie up all the loose ends."

"How? How are you going to make an innocent woman confess to five murders?" Neil demanded.

A filthy, disgusting grin touched John's lips. "Ever bury a woman up to her neck in snow...in nothing but bare skin?" John's rattlesnake eyes grinned. "The elders of this land had a way of torturing people who broke their laws. They used the cold to torment their victims. I believe Ms. Lights will agree to confess to the murders...of course, I'll have a little help." John reached into the left pocket of his coat pocket and pulled out a syringe filled with heroin. "Once Ms. Lights reaches the point of death, we'll inject this drug into her system...she'll talk... and then we'll take her from the snow and save her life."

Neil could barely believe his ears. John Richtore was insane. The old man's diseased mind was filled with insane ideas and paranoid—impractical—reasoning. Neil knew he had to be very careful. It was clear as day that John intended to kill him once a deadly body count was completed. That's why Neil left Shelia alive. He knew the woman was hiding in an attic crawl space—he knew Claude Stewart and his wife were bringing two strange women up to the ski resort. Neil had plans of his own. For the time being, he would let John continue believing that he was in complete control. The truth was, Neil did need a body count…but not in the way John expected. "How about I stick a gun to her head? That'll work."

"We'll do it my way!" John hissed. "Is that clear?" John stuffed the syringe he was holding back into his coat pocket. "The radio I have been using operates by a password. Only I have the password. Do as I say or I'll never call up the snowcat that brought you back up on this mountain, unseen and unheard. Of course," John growled, "you can try to navigate the back trail on foot…."

Neil glanced toward a coffee table that John had pushed up against the far back wall. A very high tech, sophisticated transmission CB radio stood on the table. John had been using the radio to communicate with Mandy before Mandy had hired a helicopter pilot to fly her to the ski resort. Neil needed to make contact with the man who had driven him up the back trail to the ski resort—but he could wait. He had time…plenty of time. For the time being, all Neil cared about was locating millions…hundreds of millions of dollars' worth of hidden gold. The restaurants Neil owned were miserably crumbling into dust. Neil was swamped with debt, back loan payments, and employee lawsuits. He needed to find the gold and split the scene. "You need me. That's why you brought me in, John. You need me because I know people. So, stop running your stupid mouth at me."

John glared at Neil with eyes that suddenly became very calm. Neil assumed that a helpless old man needed him. The truth was, John was going to kill Neil—no loose strings. Neil was a tool that John was using to kill five innocent people. Nothing more. Once Neil killed the intended…targets…John would simply pretend to be having a heart attack and when

Neil checked on him…*Wham!* John would shoot the man dead and then focus on forcing Bethany Lights to confess to five murders she did not commit.

Yes. That was the plan of a crazy old man who was thirsting to find a hidden goldmine filled with tons of unearthed gold—an old man consumed with a fever that was driving him to the edge of absolute, deadly insanity. Any rational, intelligent person who possessed the simplest critical thinking skills would clearly admit that John's deadly plan was filled with paranoid flaws hiding in deep craters with sharp errors. No matter. John was old and dying. He was after one final treasure hunt that would complete years of failed voyages—one miserable failed voyage after another; voyages that caused him to spiral down into a hole of insanity. "I should kill you…but sadly, the truth is, you do have contacts. Your…drug habit, dare I say, has allowed you to make valuable contacts that I am not able to make."

Neil stared at the snake sitting before him. Was John speaking the truth? Neil was far too dumb to believe that the old man might be lying. The only reason Neil managed to romance his wife's best friend was simply because the woman was a bad drug addict who depended on a sleazy no-good to bring her in loads of expensive cocaine. Ah. How the wicked fall—and John Richtore, Neil grinned inside his mind, was no exception.

"They'll all be dead before long," he told John. "Whatever you do to Bethany Lights is your deal, not mine. All I want is my cut of the gold."

"You'll get your cut. Now get back out in the storm and make sure our…targets, if you will, remain where they are," John ordered.

Silence fell in the cabin. Two worthless, slimy snakes stared at each other through soulless eyes—two snakes working on two different plans filled with deception and murder. Neil finally moved. He snatched on a black ski mask and then slid on a heavy pair of black gloves. "I'll be back in one hour," he told John and then slipped back outside into the storm.

"I'll be back in one hour...but by morning you'll see who is really in charge. And don't worry...I have no intention of killing my wife. Shelia is going to show me where the gold is...and then I'll kill her...only after she kills you. No one is leaving the ski resort alive."

Neil tucked down his head against a razor-sharp wind and began working his way through snow that was now waist deep. "The gold will be mine...no one will leave the ski resort alive...no one...."

chapter six

ethany had no idea that two men were both working to complete two different agendas that were completely insane. The poor woman had no clue that one of the men was suffering from a bout of permanent insanity and that the second man was suffering from a mind that had been destroyed by years of hard drug use. What Bethany was aware of was that the snow-battered ski resort she was being held hostage at was like being in a room filled with smoky mirrors; the scene playing before Bethany's eyes wasn't as clear as it appeared to be. *I know Shelia is scared, but there's something not right about the woman. I can't quite put my finger on what's eating at my gut. I still can't figure out who I talked to and who called me.*

Bethany glared at a secure closed door. Whoever had been standing outside of the door in the storm was no longer present. "Shelia."

"What?" Shelia snapped in a hard, annoyed voice.

Julie looked at Bethany. Bethany shook her head. *If I'm not mistaken, and I could be wrong, this woman is exhibiting symptoms of withdrawal. When I first saw her upstairs, her eyes were red...I assumed fear and fatigue had a lot to do with it. It's very clear she's very scared...but there seems to be more to Shelia Vermont than she's revealing. I also think that Shelia Vermont is far more dangerous…and clever…than she's letting on.* "Who do you think I spoke to? Who do you think called me? Who do you think created the website for this ski lodge?"

"For the umpteenth time…how should I know?" Shelia threw her hands up into the air in a manner that clearly sent irritable waves through the kitchen air. "My best friend is dead…someone is trying to kill me…and you're asking me questions that I have no possible answers to!"

"Listen, you sour custard!" Julie exploded, shocking everyone standing in the kitchen. She marched straight to Shelia and pointed a hard finger in her face. "My friend is asking sensible questions, so you better stop offering offensive answers, do you hear me? If you run your tongue toward my friend one more time, I'm going to smack your face so hard you're going to turn into a cream chowder!"

Shelia stared into a furious British face that meant business. "Get away from me—"

Julie threw back her hand and smacked Shelia across her face before anyone could stop her. Shelia stumbled backward and crashed up against a molded kitchen counter. "That's the only warning you're getting from me," Julie snapped. "Next time I'm going to tear your face off!"

Samantha began to move toward Julie, but Claude shook his head no. "Let them fight it out, Sam. I'm a bit tired of Shelia being rude too. Ain't no call for it. Bethany is just using what sense the Good Lord gave her to try and figure out what is going on. Ain't nothing in the world wrong with that." Claude eyed Shelia. "You've always seemed like a nice lady in my eyes…up until now."

"Maybe that's because Shelia has always had her drugs?" Bethany walked forward and put a caring hand on Julie's arm. "Down, tiger," she whispered.

Julie snapped her arms together. "We're sisters now, you and me," she told Bethany. "I felt an immediate bond with you from the moment we met, love. Sarah and Amanda share a bond…you and I share the same type of bond. I won't tolerate someone being rude to you."

Bethany felt tears suddenly form. *Julie truly cares about me. We are…sisters. I feel the same bond she's talking about. I can't explain it. I don't need to.* "Honey, I love you too—"

"If you ever slap me again, I'll kill you!" Shelia yelled, attacking Julie with her words like a tiger tearing into raw meat. "How dare you!"

Julie unfolded her arms. "Stand back, everyone…."

"No, honey." Bethany held Julie back. "Shelia seems to be going through withdrawal. I'm assuming she used up the last of her drugs while hiding."

"Drugs?" Samantha asked in a confused voice. "No. Shelia is a nice…well, from the few times Claude and I met her, she seemed to be a very pleasant and honest woman." Samantha didn't want to admit to herself that she might have read Shelia in the wrong light. Usually, Samantha was spot on at looking into a person's heart.

"Yes, I'm afraid Shelia might be a drug user, Samantha," Bethany told her new friend in a steady tone. "What is it, Shelia? You're certainly not this ill because you're hungry for marijuana. No. You're addicted to something far heavier. Cocaine, maybe?"

"You think you're so smart," Shelia began to plow into Bethany.

"No, I'm thinking that this ski resort has a lot of mirages attached to it," Bethany informed Shelia. "Your best friend is dead. Your husband is absent from the scene. Your dad is supposedly dead. I made contact with someone who invited me to this ski resort—someone who seemed to have made a website that showed this ski resort in good standing, which tells me someone does want to dedicate time and energy into fixing up this place." Bethany glanced around and then looked back at Shelia. "The website had the words 'Closed for

Renovation Until Further Notice' posted across the top in large red letters. You claim you know nothing about the website."

"I don't!" Shelia yelled. "How many times do I have to tell you that?"

"Maybe you don't," Bethany agreed, "but someone made the website in question, and I certainly spoke with a woman who claimed to be you, and a woman claiming to be you called my cabin the same day Julie and I decided to visit the ski lodge and offer a helping hand. So, can you tell me who I spoke to...who called me...who is out in the storm? No. You can't. Why? Because I honestly believe you are not aware of what's going on. But that doesn't mean you're telling the entire truth."

"Drop dead!" Shelia snapped. Julie bawled up her fist. Shelia flinched some. "Leave me alone!"

"Shelia, if I'm not mistaken, and I could be...I believe you wanted to buy this ski resort in order to start running drugs. I believe your friend might have been part of your scheme." Bethany glanced around the kitchen again. The wood-burning stove was struggling to keep the kitchen warm, but at least the kitchen was managing to hold in life-saving heat.

"You're delusional...go see a psychiatrist," Shelia growled at Bethany.

"You never told us what you did for a living?" Bethany asked. "Did you have a career before you found out your husband was being unfaithful?"

"That's a mighty good question, Shelia," Claude said in a stern tone. "You told us that you told your old man you wanted to escape from the world after finding out your husband had been messing around with a no-good woman. But before that...I wonder, what were you doing? Where did you live? Work?" Claude walked over to the wood-burning stove with his rifle in hand. Samantha was standing close to the wood-burning stove. He stood close to his wife and waited for Shelia to speak.

Shelia felt her mind start to race. Again, she felt like she was becoming a trapped animal. "My personal life is none of your business...but if you must know, I helped my husband manage his restaurants. I have a degree in business. Mandy and I met while I was in college...Boston University."

Bethany grew silent for a minute. *What's the point in trying to back Shelia Vermont into a tight corner? What am I expecting of this woman? So what, this woman is a drug addict? So what if she bought this ski resort with the intention to start running illegal drugs? My life is in Snow Falls, not up on Ice Mountain. All I should be concerned about is escaping this mountain alive with Julie, Samantha, and Claude.* "Well, Shelia, your past, present... and future...aren't any of my concern. It's clear that you're hiding a lot of facts, but I personally don't care. I could stand here all day and grill you, but what would be the point?" Bethany focused on Claude. "Claude, our purpose should be to survive this storm and get down off this mountain."

"Yeah, I see your point," Claude said, nodding his head. He eyed Shelia with sour eyes and then focused on the back door. "Winds are worse than before. We wouldn't last long out in that storm. We best stay in this kitchen to first light and then see what we can do. Ain't nobody getting in here without eating a bullet supper."

"I agree...," Bethany began to say, but then her mind slammed up against a stop sign. *Wait...Shelia said Mandy arrived by helicopter. How did she communicate with her friend? Claude said the communication radio Shelia has is broken. When and how was the radio broken? Had to be before Mandy arrived before Claude knew the radio was broken. So how...how did Shelia communicate with her friend? Maybe Mr. Richtore set a date for Mandy to arrive? Maybe no communication between Shelia and Mandy took place...but...* Bethany bit down on her lower lip as her mind began to nibble at a few nagging questions. *Mr.*

Richtore visited my coffee shop…left…went to the hunting lodge… and from there Claude and Samantha used the snowcat to take him to the ski resort. They brought Shelia's husband down from the ski resort when they left…Mandy Pacemore was not on the scene yet…but when the woman arrived, she arrived by helicopter. Why? Why didn't she have Claude and Samantha use the snowcat to drive her up to the ski resort? Could it be the woman didn't want to be seen? Or could it be she was…making a private delivery of some sort? And why did she arrive only after Shelia's husband left?

"What are you thinking, love?" Julie asked. Boy, was she ever hungry. A double cheeseburger with a plate of salty fries and a chocolate milkshake sure sounded good. Julie had to admit that at times her appetite could match her cousin Amanda's appetite. Thinking on an empty stomach was tough business.

"Shelia, why did Mandy Pacemore arrive by helicopter? Why didn't she hire Claude and Samantha to drive her up to the ski resort in the snowcat?" Bethany demanded. "And why did your husband leave right before your friend arrived? Seems a little…suspicious, now that I think about it."

"I told you why my husband left!" Shelia hollered at Bethany.

"Yes, you did." Bethany's face transformed into a deep canyon of doubt. "Shelia, could it be that you're glad your best friend is dead?"

"What? You're—" Shelia began to erupt.

"Could it be…Mandy Pacemore was your husband's mistress?" Bethany continued, standing her ground on firm legs. "Maybe? Maybe not? I'm sure all the pieces of the puzzle will fall into place eventually. All I do know is that right now, I believe you're not as upset about your friend being dead as you're making out. I've seen you look toward the freezer a few times…a few times I saw bitterness enter your eyes."

"Drop dead!"

"I told you to watch your tongue!" Julie bawled her small hands into two mean fists. "I'm going to teach you—"

"Down girl," Claude ordered Julie in a stern tone. "I would let you two fight it out, but…." Claude looked into Bethany's eyes. "Keep talking."

Bethany lifted a tired hand and rubbed her eyes. "I noticed that Shelia didn't appear overly upset when she told us her dad had been killed. She cried a few tears over Mandy Pacemore and tossed a quick guilt wardrobe that was quickly removed. She also doesn't seem overly upset that her marriage is about to end. As a matter of fact," Bethany said, shaking her head, "Shelia seems anxious for her marriage to end."

"You're a piece of crap!" Shelia hollered at Bethany. "Do you hear me!"

Bethany ignored Shelia's insult. "Shelia is exhibiting signs of withdrawal…her behavior is common for someone who hasn't had a hit in a while. My…husband was addicted to pain relievers. Whenever he ran out, he became very irritable if not hostile until his prescription could be filled." Bethany turned her back to Shelia and pointed at the walk-in freezer. "Mandy Pacemore was killed without wearing a coat. That tells me she was killed when the lodge was warm enough to walk around without a coat—" A deep groan left Bethany's mouth. "Why didn't I put two and two together earlier? I could kick myself!"

"What is it? Speak your mind," Claude demanded.

Bethany spun around. "Shelia, you said someone shot your dad while you two were checking the cabins, right?"

"Yes—"

"Which means he died first, because after Mandy Pacemore was attacked, you ran upstairs, not outside—and your dad wasn't present," Bethany pointed out.

"I…well, yes…," Shelia quickly stuttered.

"You're wearing a sweater…you were outside with your

dad in the snow when he was shot, right?" Bethany asked. Shelia gritted her teeth and reluctantly nodded yes. "So why did you come back to the lodge and remove your coat? Seems to me you would have kept your coat. And speaking of your coat, I didn't see any coats in the front room. Where is your coat?"

"In the apartment—" Shelia began to scream but stopped. Realizing she had allowed her tongue to speak a fatal mistake, she threw her eyes down at the floor. "Leave me alone!"

"So, your dad was killed...yet, you put your coat in an upstairs apartment and then went downstairs to chat with your friend?" Bethany shook her head. "No. Something more is going on than meets the eye."

"I told you to leave me alone!" Shelia growled.

Bethany looked into the faces of three worried people. "Bethany," Claude said, "you might just be hitting on a few pieces of hidden gold." Claude's face turned very angry in the weak light the lantern sitting on a round wooden table was throwing out. "You best start talking, woman," he snapped at Shelia in a hard voice, "because my wife's life is in danger, and I don't appreciate that fact one bit. I also don't appreciate being made a fool of!"

Shelia slowly raised her eyes, looked into Claude's face, and then without any warning bolted out of the kitchen on panicked legs. Bethany shook her head. "Go get her, Claude, before she ends up dead. Whoever the killer is, I'm certain he isn't going to let Shelia leave this ski resort alive, either."

Confusion is an awful enemy. Combine that enemy with a group of people who were attached to different agendas, and well, you get a whole lot of question marks lingering in the air that decimate practical problem-solving solutions. But isn't that the way murder always plays out in the end? Bethany thought so as Claude dragged Shelia back into a dimly lit kitchen. "All right, Shelia," Bethany said in a tough voice, "the communication radio that is supposedly broken… where is it?"

Claude aimed his rifle at Shelia. "I done fired one warning shot at you in the dining room. The next shot will be aimed directly at you. Start talking!"

"Claude…you know the radio is broken," Shelia began to whimper.

"Perhaps a radio that you want Claude to believe is broken, but I'm certain there is another communication radio hidden somewhere." Bethany felt a tinge of hope touch her heart. If she was right in assuming a functional radio was hidden at some unknown location, that meant there was a chance to call out for help.

"I don't—"

"Your dad isn't dead, Shelia!" Bethany snapped so hard that Shelia stumbled backward. Claude grabbed her arm. "If someone shot your dad out in the open, then why didn't that person shoot you? You claim you put your dad's body in cabin number 4 and ran back to the lodge…if there was a hidden shooter hiding outside, that person would have certainly gunned you down before you reached the lodge… probably while you were dragging your dad's body into cabin number 4. I should have put two and two together earlier, but to be honest…I'm very scared. My mind is running in a hundred different directions and I'm having to chew on what I believe is important enough to investigate."

"Don't kick yourself," Claude told Bethany. "You don't see the rest of us taking the role of 'Columbo.'"

"Claude is right, Bethany," Samantha said in a quick voice. "We're trapped in a desperate situation and all of us are mighty stressed." Samantha hurried to Claude. "If there is a working radio—"

"I know," Claude told his wife in a quick voice. "Question is…how do we find it?" Claude threw his eyes at Shelia. "Where is the radio!"

"My dad was shot…right before my eyes…honest."

"Let's assume you're telling the truth," Bethany cut Shelia off. "Why did the killer let you live?" Bethany shook her head. "Maybe you and the killer had a plan of some sort? And maybe, Shelia, you came back to the lodge to lure your friend into a deadly trap…and in the end…the killer ended up turning on you? And right now, you're in panic mode… trying to figure out a way to make yourself look innocent."

"That's not true…." It was clear to Shelia that she was in serious trouble. Trying to make a run for it certainly didn't help her case.

"Where is the radio, girl?" Samantha marched forward and snagged Shelia's wrist. "You better talk or I'm going to throw you out into that storm and let you freeze to death, do you hear me!"

"You better speak the truth," Julie added, speaking in a way that told Shelia she was ready for a good fight.

Bethany waited for Shelia to talk. When Shelia dropped her eyes and looked down at a cold wooden floor, she shook her head. "I don't think—"

Before Bethany could finish her words, she saw the image of Sarah Spencer enter her mind. Sarah was standing in a rainy alley in Los Angeles looking down at a dead body. The Back Alley Killer had struck again and Sarah was on the case. *Sarah always managed to keep her thoughts organized and functional. She never panicked and she never tried to chase a million leads all at once. I need to slow down and focus. I'm running too fast and too hard. I know there's more taking place at this awful ski resort than meets the eye, but I have to focus on one door at a time. If I don't slow down, I'm liable to kick open a wrong door and encounter a deadly killer. Now think—take every word Shelia has spoken, evaluate each word, and find a lead that's worth chasing.*

"What is it?" Claude asked Bethany. "What are you chewing on now?"

Bethany walked over to the walk-in freezer, touched the outside of the rusted door attached to the it, and then closed her eyes. *Of course...* Bethany let out a heavy, painful sigh. *Mandy Pacemore would have needed a way to communicate with the outside world. Shelia confessed that Mandy Pacemore didn't have a set day to leave...so how would she have made contact with the outside world if the only radio at the ski resort was broken? Goodness...how did Sarah do it...being a detective for all of those years...solving all those murder cases? My mind is just now playing catch-up.*

"Bethany, speak your mind before I go mad," Claude demanded. "What in the world are you thinking?"

Bethany turned away from the walk-in freezer. "There is another communication radio, Shelia. You told us that Mandy Pacemore was prepared to stay at the ski resort for a long period of time and didn't have a set day to leave. The woman arrived by helicopter. How would she have called out to the outside world or...even called Claude and Samantha if that's the exit route she would have chosen?"

"Well, I'll be!" Claude smacked the kitchen table he was standing next to with his left hand so hard the table nearly collapsed. "Bethany, you hit the nail on the head!" Claude handed Samantha his rifle and grabbed Shelia by her arms. "You best talk, do you hear me!" he yelled in Shelia's face.

"You better talk!" Samantha joined in. Samantha was so angry, steam seemed to be coming out of her ears.

Shelia simply broke down and began to cry. "It's not what you think...it wasn't supposed to be like this! Please...let me go...let me go...!"

Claude pushed Shelia toward the walk-in freezer. "You want to join your friend? Talk!" he yelled.

Shelia locked her eyes on the walk-in freezer as cold tears rolled down her cheeks. "Are you happy now, Mandy? Are you? You ruined my marriage and my life, but at least you're dead!" she screamed. "You're dead! My plan may have failed, but at least you're dead! Neil killed you!" Shelia began beating the door of the walk-in freezer with two trembling fists. "Before it's over, I'm going to kill Neil for what he did to me! Do you hear me? You both are going to rot together! All of you...even Dad!"

Bethany watched Shelia hit the walk-in freezer door over and over again and then collapse down onto her knees and throw her hands over a red, angry, defeated face.

"Shelia, where is the radio?" she asked, speaking in a gentle tone. There was no sense in being tough with a broken woman anymore. It was clear that Shelia had thrown in the towel.

"I need a hit...I need a hit." Shelia began shaking all over. "I need my heroin. That's how Neil always controlled me. He got me addicted to heroin...I thought he loved me, but he betrayed me...even when he promised to kill Mandy and come back to me...he betrayed me...."

"Stupid outsiders!" Claude barked. "Now do you see why I don't want to turn our hunting lodge into some sissy marriage retreat, Sam? Outsiders bring nothing but trouble." Claude spit on the kitchen floor. "Drugs...murder...lies... makes my stomach sick. Back in the older days, a man wouldn't put up with this nonsense!"

"I...just have one question," Julie said. "I still don't understand why Bethany and I were tricked into taking a holiday at this awful ski resort."

"I'm sure Shelia knows," Bethany told Julie. "But now isn't the time to try and find out." Bethany walked over to Shelia and bent down. "Neil, your husband, he's the one out in the storm, right?" Shelia reluctantly nodded. "Is there anyone else?"

"My dad...but he's dead. Neil really did shoot him...I... watched...we were at cabin number 4...Neil shot Dad...he dragged his body into the cabin...." Shelia refused to look up at Bethany. "Dad is a dangerous man...he had to die. He...wanted to take all the gold for himself. Neil and I...we worked out our problems. Neil agreed to kill Dad and Mandy...we were going to hide their bodies, but then you two came onto the scene somehow. Neil talked me into agreeing to help him frame you for the murders...but then he turned on me. He tried to kill me. I barely escaped with my life."

"Maybe he let you live," Bethany pointed out. "Maybe right now your husband—and I could be wrong—is going to try and kill everyone, leaving only you alive. He knows you must be hungering for your drug...maybe he's giving you time to completely break down in order to control you."

"And blame all the murders on you too," Julie added in an important tone.

"Exactly," Bethany said, nodding. "Your husband is keeping you alive for a reason."

"It's the gold...Neil wants all the gold for himself. I...know where the gold is, do does...did...Dad. Dad has to be dead. I saw Neil shoot him," Shelia cried. She ran her hands over her face like a desperate inmate trying to escape from a prison. "Neil believes the gold is in the form of stolen gold bars...the gold is raw...Dad made Neil believe the gold was already prepared to be hauled away if someone found it. It was all a lie...Dad lured Neil to this mountain to kill him for what he did to me...at least that's what he told me. It was all a lie...Dad...he wanted us all dead...everyone...I found his journal."

"Stupid outsiders!" Claude yelled again. "All the outsiders bring to this land is trouble!" Claude spit on the floor again. "Gold...murder...lies...betrayal...this person has this plan, that person has that plan...this person does this, this person does that...makes me sick!"

Bethany understood Claude's anger. It did seem like

everyone connected to Shelia Vermont had created a deadly plan of their own. Each person, Bethany assumed, had personal reasons for attempting to murder innocent people for a bunch of silly gold. "Shelia, where is the radio?" she asked.

"I don't know. The radio was right here in this kitchen, but then...it went missing on the day Neil shot Dad," Shelia confessed. "I...." Shelia raised her tear-stained eyes. "The scene was supposed to look authentic. That's why I showed Claude the broken radio...no one was supposed to know that Mandy arrived by helicopter."

"Are you that stupid, girl?" Samantha snapped. "You and your lousy husband decided to kill two people and hide the bodies? Claude and me brought your dad up here. Don't you think we would have eventually asked questions?"

"Yes...but...."

"But you were going to kill your husband and blame the murders on him, right?" Bethany asked Shelia. "I want the truth."

"Yes!" Shelia screamed in agony. "I was going to kill Neil and blame the murders on him...you and your stupid British friend showed up on the scene unexpected."

"How did your husband get back up on this mountain?" Bethany asked.

"He hired a man to drive him back up using the back trail...happy?" Shelia grabbed her face again. "Enough questions...I can't stand it anymore!"

Outside the kitchen door, Neil narrowed a pair of deadly eyes. "You've just marked yourself for death," he hissed. "It's time to die...all of you. I can't afford to keep anyone alive any longer. My plans have just changed." Neil backed away into a thick darkness and hurried toward a wooden shack standing in the far distance. A full crate of old dynamite was resting in the shack. "I'll blow you all to pieces. I'll just have to make the old man tell me where the gold is. Since he likes the idea of torturing people, maybe he won't mind if I torture him."

Bethany had no idea that Neil was planning to blow the kitchen into bits of kindle. "All right, everyone, listen. We've been in this kitchen for a couple of hours and so far, Shelia's husband hasn't tried to harm us. Earlier I felt as if someone was standing outside the back door, but my feeling went away...so here's the plan. We're going to go out into the storm—"

"Into the storm?" Samantha quickly asked in a worried voice. "Bethany, the winds will kill us. I've lived through many a winter and—"

"Samantha, hear me out," Bethany pleaded.

"Hear her out, Sam," Claude barked. "Bethany has brains in her head. We need to listen to her...she ain't no flapping fish." Claude nodded at Bethany. "What's your plan?"

"We put out the lantern and leave the kitchen under the cover of absolute darkness. We work our way to cabin number 4. My gut is telling me there's something special about that cabin." Bethany bit down on her lower lip. *I'm risking everyone's life by taking them out into the storm, but my gut is telling me that we need to investigate cabin number 4. My gut is also starting to worry that the safety this kitchen is offering everyone is going to come to an end real quick.* "Shelia, we're about to find out if your dad is really dead or not."

"You heard Bethany. Let's get the lantern put out and get ready to go out into the storm," Claude barked. "We'll leave the kitchen in pairs. Sam, you're at my side. Bethany, you and Julie are a team. Shelia...you're going in the freezer for the time being."

"What?" Shelia began to panic. "No, you can't—"

"I can and I will," Claude hollered. "You set your friend up to die, so you're going to sit with her until we get this mess all figured out!" Claude moved to Shelia and snatched the woman up with a hard hand. "I had you figured all wrong. I thought you were a decent sort…Bethany, open the freezer door!"

Bethany did as ordered without the slightest hesitation. *What's good for the goose is good for the gander. Besides, we can't risk taking Shelia with us. She's an unstable threat.* "In you go."

Before Shelia could object, Claude pushed her into the freezer. "Sam, bring her the lantern…ain't right to leave her in the dark. Best leave the lantern for her instead of putting it out." Samantha grabbed a lantern off a worn-down wooden table and placed it just inside the walk-in freezer door. "Sit tight!"

"I hope Neil kills you all!" Shelia screamed out in rage.

Claude rolled his eyes and slammed the freezer door shut, not realizing that by locking Shelia inside, he was actually saving the woman's life. "All right, let's go," he ordered. "In pairs, like I said."

Bethany looked at Julie. Julie simply braced herself for a nightmare—a nightmare that was lurking just outside the kitchen door. *Here we go…into the mouth of darkness. There's no turning back now.*

chapter seven

I'm going to freeze to death! Bethany felt razor winds cut through her body like the blade of a sharp sword even though she was bundled up in a thick winter coat and a protective muffler hat. *The hat…my coat…the winter pants…my boots…worthless against this wind. It wasn't this cold when we arrived…and the snow is so deep. How can we walk through all of these deep snowdrifts? I feel like I'm drowning in a sea of dark snow. I can't see anything…the snow is up to my waist…the winds are so strong I can't even raise my head…I feel like my body is turning to ice.*

Bethany wasn't the only one being battered by an icy fist. Julie, Samantha, and Claude were all moaning inside their hearts. "This is no good…we have to turn back!" Claude finally yelled. "The winds will kill us!"

"We can't turn back!" Bethany screamed, desperately holding on to the back wall of the ski resort as if she were drowning and the wall was a life raft. "We have to get to cabin number 4! We have to locate the emergency radio!" *But how? How are we going to make it through this storm? It's impossible! We're in complete white-out conditions. This is suicide!*

Claude struggled to hold on to Samantha's hand as he inched forward through a deep snowdrift, hanging on to the back wall of the ski resort like a man searching for light in a dark cave. Suddenly his hand came upon a door. "I found a door!" he hollered over the screaming winds. Without wasting a second, Claude began fighting with a rusted doorknob. To his relief, the doorknob turned. He drew back his right leg and kicked open a heavy door. "Everyone get inside, now!"

Bethany wanted to force her legs to keep moving through the storm, but for the time being, she was done for. Instead of arguing with Claude, she grabbed Julie's hand and dived into a small room that once served as a back office. Julie tumbled into the room after her. Samantha followed…and then Claude scrambled in as if he were being chased by a grizzly bear. Claude quickly handed Samantha his rifle and began fighting to close the office door. Bethany ran to Claude and offered her assistance. "Almost there…winds are so strong…keeping pushing, Claude."

Claude let out a painful holler and, using the last of his strength, managed to close the office door with Bethany's help and then collapsed down into a hard, cold, wood floor. "Whew…I haven't been this tired in a long time."

Samantha crashed down next to her husband. "I don't think I have the means to move another inch," she moaned. "I can't even shake the snow off me."

Bethany had to remind herself that Claude and Samantha weren't spring chickens anymore—and neither was she. Being a woman in her early forties was far different than being twenty-one. "I can't see. Samantha, do you have the flashlight?"

Samantha managed to reach into a frozen coat pocket and pull out a flashlight. "Here, honey, take it," she said through streams of white ice.

Bethany took the flashlight. "I think we're in a back office. I'll keep the light low."

Julie plunged down next to Claude and waited for

Bethany to turn on the flashlight. "You Americans are strange creatures. In England we enjoy a peaceful tea and crumpet without raising a fuss. Here in America, it seems all you Americans are out to kill each other."

Claude felt a grin touch his exhausted face. He enjoyed it when Julie fussed—he found her British accent brilliant and amusing, even though he would never admit such a thing. "Sure seems that way, doesn't it?"

"Yes, it does." Julie nodded and then plopped her chin down onto Claude's shoulder. "Much better."

Claude reached up and patted Julie's arm. "It's going to be okay," he promised Julie.

Bethany quickly reached out her hands and began investigating four wooden walls. If the room she was standing in had a window, she wouldn't turn on the flashlight. But as it seemed, the room was windowless. Bethany wanted to be sure. "No windows," she finally said, keeping her voice low, and then clicked on the weak flashlight. Julie, Samantha, and Claude all followed a cold, gray light around a bare room. "This is the room that stands behind the front counter…the front room is just beyond that door," Bethany whispered. "We didn't get very far, I'm afraid."

"Far? We made it maybe fifty yards." Claude shook his head. "It felt like we walked ten miles. It's like that when the snow is deep and the winds are sharp enough to cut a man in half."

"One thing is for certain…we can't go back out," Samantha pointed out. "We'll die. Besides, I don't have the strength to move even if I did want to go back out into the storm. Our little trip we just took…drained me. I'm done for. Turn me over and stick a fork in my backside."

"Same here," Claude admitted in a voice that was clearly exhausted. "A man knows his limits. I know better than to try and go back out into the storm. After we rest, we need to try and get back to the kitchen…oh…no. We barricaded the dining room door!" Claude kicked himself. "We'll have to break down the door or go back around…which means we'll have to go back outside."

"Claude, we need to find the radio," Bethany insisted. "If you and Samantha can't go back outside…and I understand, honestly I do…then I'll go alone. Julie can stay here with you."

"No, love," Julie vehemently objected. "We're staying together."

"We're all staying together," Samantha demanded. "Bethany, you're a brave soul, but let's face it, even if we could go back into the storm, what good would it do? There's no promise that the radio we're looking for will be in cabin number 4. As far as we know, the radio could be in the upstairs apartment…or hidden anywhere."

"I know, Samantha." Bethany clicked off the flashlight, allowing complete darkness to take control of the back office room. "My gut…my heart…is telling me—no, insisting that I need to go to cabin number 4." Bethany felt her legs begin to tremble some. She needed to sit down. *This is so hopeless. All this effort…my mind trying to play Nancy Drew…risking death to find a missing radio…what for? It would make more sense to just… hide.* A heavy despair filled with pessimistic poison entered Bethany's heart. She slumped down next to Julie and bowed her head.

"Are you all right, love?" Julie whispered.

"No," Bethany confessed. "Julie, I dared to begin a new life in Snow Falls. So far, my new life has been a difficult rollercoaster ride. I've been struggling to stay on track, but it hasn't been easy. At times I feel like throwing in the towel and moving to North Carolina. I know that would make my mother happy. My mother would be thrilled if I moved to North Carolina and began attending her weekly garden club meetings."

"Then why don't you move to North Carolina, honey?" Samantha asked.

Bethany slowly raised her eyes and peered into a dark room that felt like an icy crypt. "When my husband was alive, he controlled me." She spoke in a broken voice. "My husband never physically abused me, but he hit me with cruel words and hateful intent on a daily basis. I endured…. What choice did I have? In the part of the world I lived in, a wife, abused or not, never ripped a Band-Aid off her marriage and showed the world painful wounds. A wife simply…endured."

"Where I come from, if a man is cruel to a woman, you take him out and shoot him!" Claude told Bethany in an angry tone. "A woman just doesn't…endure, like you say."

"Claude, I come from a completely different world than you," Bethany explained as horrible memories began scratching at her heart with sharp, cruel claws. "Anyway…" Bethany said, struggling to hold her pain at bay, "after my husband died…and that's a very long story in itself…I decided to start a new life. I decided to fight. As scared as I felt inside…terrified, to be perfectly honest…I chose to move to Snow Falls, Alaska and begin a new life."

"Why did you choose Snow Falls?" Samantha asked.

"Because once, long ago, my daddy and I traveled to Snow Falls to pick up the body of his brother. As sad as the trip was…the trip was also turned into a precious memory. I was able to spend time with Daddy in a way that I had never been able to do before…. It's difficult to explain." Bethany felt a tear sting her eye. "I wanted…needed…to return to a place where I felt I could heal and be at peace. A place that once brought me happiness, even if that happiness only lasted for a few short days. Snow Falls…well, Snow Falls somehow became a lighthouse in a very dark storm."

"I heard there was some killings there," Claude told Bethany. "There's been lots of killings in that town. A woman named Sarah—"

"Sarah Spencer," Julie said, cutting Claude off.

"First name is right; last name sounds off."

"Sarah married Conrad Spencer," Bethany informed Claude.

"Well, be that as it may, I heard talk that the woman was a curse," Claude stated. "Never seen so many people die in one little town before that woman arrived."

And when I arrived in Snow Falls, the killings began again. And now look at me. I'm trapped in a frozen tomb fighting for my life. As Charlie Brown would say...good grief. "Claude... Samantha—" Bethany began but stopped when her ears caught a sound coming from the front room.

"Listen," she whispered in a quick voice, "someone is in the front room."

Julie, Samantha, and Claude all tuned their ears toward the front room. They heard footsteps. "Easy," Claude whispered in a careful voice. He skillfully placed the rifle he was holding into an offensive position and slowly struggled to his legs. "Bethany—"

Bethany pulled a cold Glock 17 out of the right pocket of her coat. She switched off the safety. "I'm ready, Claude," she whispered. "Tell me what to do."

"Sam, when I tell you, yank open the door. Julie, your job will be to aim the flashlight at whoever is in the front room. Bethany...aim straight and shoot fast. Don't matter who is in the front room...we're shooting that person down. Could be the killer...."

Bethany wanted to object, but she didn't. Who else but the killer would be prowling around the front room? Shelia's dad? Maybe. Whoever was in the front room obviously wasn't a friend. *A woman is dead. We can't risk trying to play nice. Claude is right. At this point, it's kill or be killed.* "All right, Claude. I'm with you."

"Sam...Julie...get in place."

Julie helped Samantha stand up. Samantha reached out,

squeezed Claude's hand, and then tiptoed to a closed door on silent legs. Bethany quickly handed Julie the flashlight she was holding. "Ready?" she whispered.

"Love, the next time we need to take a holiday, we're going to O'Mally's," Julie whispered back.

"I couldn't agree—"

Claude grabbed Bethany's arm and pulled her next to the closed door. He told her to hush and get ready to act. "Aim straight and shoot fast." Claude nodded.

"Ready?" Samantha whispered. She raised her right hand and grabbed a frozen doorknob. "On the count of three." Julie tensed up and prepared to snatch on the flashlight. There was no turning back.

"One…."

Bethany checked the gun she was holding. *Please Lord,* she prayed.

"Two," Samantha whispered.

Whoever is in the front room is about to die…please, Lord, let that person be the killer. Bethany made sure her trigger finger was prepared for action. Claude drew in a deep breath. "When that door opens, start shooting," he whispered in Bethany's ear.

"Three!" Samantha bravely yanked open the office door. Julie snapped on the flashlight she was holding and threw the light directly out of the door. Claude and Bethany charged through the door like brave soldiers storming a bullet-torn beach. A tall man wearing a black ski suit spun around and then bolted toward the entry door on lightning-fast legs.

"You there…stop!" Claude yelled and then took aim at the fleeing man and fired off a quick shot. Unfortunately, he took a quick nosedive toward the entry door right as Claude fired. A sizzling bullet whizzed past the man's head, missing him by mere inches. Bethany swung around Claude's left shoulder and fired off three clean bullets. Each bullet struck the entry door just above the man's head. Before Claude could fire off another shot, the man vanished into the storm. Claude ran to the front door as fast as he could. Bethany followed like a faithful friend. Claude threw his eyes out into a frozen darkness. "Gone...into the storm," he grumbled.

Bethany peered out into the storm. All she saw was blinding snow screaming out of a dark, deadly mouth. "Close the door...hurry." Claude quickly helped Bethany close and lock the entry door. "Claude, Shelia told us her husband was somewhat fat and not very tall. The man who just fled was tall and lanky...and fast."

Claude looked into Bethany's eyes as Samantha and Julie hurried into the front room. "We got another killer on the loose? Is that what you're saying?" he asked in a strained voice.

"I don't know. But it does appear we have another player in the game." Bethany turned and looked toward the stone fireplace standing in the front room. A dying fire was barely gasping for air. *The man Claude and I just encountered couldn't be Shelia's husband. According to Shelia, her husband is fat and somewhat short...good grief, now there's another dangerous man running loose.* Bethany continued to stare at the fireplace as her mind fought to calm down.

"The man we shot at got away...Bethany and I both missed him. Fella was faster than a wounded fox," Claude told Samantha and Julie in a worried voice. "We got another rat loose in the storm."

"What do we do, Claude?" Samantha begged.

"That entry door was locked from the inside, but the fella who got away snatched the door open without fussing with the lock...I guess we need to find out how he got inside this lodge." Claude nodded toward a wooden staircase. "We're back to square one. We best get upstairs and have a look around."

Back at square one. Yes. That sums up my life. Bethany dropped her shoulders. What else could she do?

Outside in the storm, Neil was preparing a crate full of dynamite for action.

"You want to check the attic crawl space Shelia was hiding in?" Claude asked.

Bethany nodded. "Yes. I may find nothing...then again, I may find something." Bethany quickly ran her eyes up and down a dark hallway. *Back at square one. Back in the same upstairs hallway as before. No closer to hope than before.* "I'll hurry."

Before Claude could offer any objection, Bethany hurried into the room Shelia had stumbled out of earlier. Julie and Samantha began to follow, but Claude shook his head. "Sam, let her go," he said in a low, stern voice. "We'll stay right here and guard the hallway. Our eyes will just have to adjust to the dark. Bethany will need the flashlight."

Julie stuck her head into a dark, cold room and watched a beam of weak light run toward an open closet door. "Be careful," she pleaded.

Bethany dashed into a small closet and looked up. A single metal bar ran across her head. "The bar must be for people to hang their clothes." Bethany aimed the flashlight she was holding up. Light splashed onto a small square hole sitting in the closet ceiling. "No ladder...so how did Shelia manage to get up into the crawl space?" Bethany examined the length and width of the closet with focused eyes. "She could have spider-walked up the closet...or used the bar...the question is, how am I going to get up into the attic crawl space?"

Determined not to give up, Bethany shoved the flashlight she was holding into the front pocket of her coat and then braced her arms against the closet walls. "I'm going to spider-walk up as far as I can and then when I'm able, I'll use the bar as leverage to push myself up." Drawing in a deep breath, Bethany prayed for strength and then went to work. She placed her right boot against the closet wall and then, using her arms to lift her body, she managed to hoist her left leg off the floor and plant it on the opposite closet wall. *I'm too old for this...I'm not sixteen, for crying out loud...but if Shelia managed to get up there...then so will I.* Biting down on her lip, Bethany forced her right boot to move in fluent motion with a pair of sweaty hands. Slowly—painfully—she managed to spider-walk up the closet just far enough to throw her right hand up into a dark hole. "Got it...now...I need to put my feet on the bar..." Feeling what appeared to be a strong piece of old wood, Bethany took a second to secure a firm grip with her right hand and then, using every bit of strength she had, pulled her body up just enough to allow her boots to land firmly on a rusted old bar. *Now all I have to do is hoist myself up into the hole...goodness, I feel like a silly sixteen-year-old.*

With weak, exhausted arms, Bethany pulled herself up into a cramped dark hole, using her legs to assist her while hoping and praying the bar she was standing on wouldn't give out and crash down. Using extreme caution, Bethany crawled up into the hole, pulling her body onto old attic boards, and then whipped out a flashlight from her coat pocket. "Very tight in here...but there's room to move..." Bethany examined the cramped space that matched Shelia's description. "I don't see...wait...what's that?" Bethany aimed the flashlight at what appeared to be a small piece of ripped paper stuck to a piece of rusted nail. She quickly fished out a gloved hand and retrieved the piece of paper. "Nathaniel Taylor...and there seems to be a phone number...but only the last four numbers..."

Bethany shoved the piece of paper into her pocket and continued to scan the crawl space. "Ah..." A gray, cold beam of light struck what appeared to be a used syringe. "Looks like Shelia decided to shoot up." Bethany shook her head and then, feeling as if she had adequately examined the crawl space, began the difficult task of lowering her body back down into the closet. "Easy…almost there…"

When Julie saw Bethany step out of the closet, she rushed forward. "Did you find anything, love?"

"I think so." Bethany took Julie's hand and hurried back to Claude and Samantha. She handed over the flashlight to Samantha. "I found a piece of paper…look." Bethany pulled the ripped piece of paper she found and shoved it in front of the flashlight.

"Nathaniel…Taylor…and…four numbers…" Claude spoke in a thoughtful voice.

"Could be the last four digits to a telephone number?" Bethany suggested. "We need to go back down to the kitchen and demand Shelia tell us who Nathaniel Taylor is. We'll just have to break through the dining room door instead of going back outside and—"

Kaboom!

A loud, violent explosion tore through the lodge like a hideous snow beast letting out a fierce scream. The force of the explosion rocked the upstairs with such power that Bethany lost her balance and crashed down onto a cold floor. Julie followed. Claude grabbed Samantha and tried to keep his legs under him but failed. He hit the floor with his wife like a pile of wet rocks as pieces of the hallway ceiling began cracking and falling, striking everyone on the head. Claude threw his arms over Samantha's head and ducked down.

"What was that?" Julie cried, shielding her face from falling debris. "Did a gas tank explode?"

"That was dynamite," Claude yelled. "Shelia's husband is trying to blast us out of here!"

Bethany dared to raise her head. As she did, a piece of falling cciling struck her cheek, creating an ugly gash. Bethany winced in pain and quickly covered her wound with a gloved hand. Blood began soaking into a snow-soaked glove. *Great. Now I'm bleeding!* "We need to get out of here!"

Julie saw Bethany cover her face. "Love, you're hurt." Without any concern for her own safety, Julie crawled over to Bethany. "Let me see. Samantha, put your flashlight on Bethany's face." Samantha quickly did as Julie asked. Julie carefully removed Bethany's hand from the wound attached to her face. "Oh dear...you have a bad cut...keep pressure on it."

Claude whipped a brown rag out of his coat pocket. "I used this rag to check the oil in the cat with...ignore the oil and put the rag over your cut."

Bethany accepted the oily rag Claude was holding. She placed the rag over her wound. *I doubt I'll get an infection. It wouldn't matter if I did. I have more serious matters to worry about.* "The explosion sounded like—"

"The kitchen," Claude confirmed. "Let's go." Claude climbed to his legs. "Sam, can you walk?"

"I can walk," Samantha promised. The tough old woman got to her feet. "Shelia might be dead. We need to check on her."

Julie helped Samantha stand up. "I hate to admit it, love, but you're right," she told Samantha, her voice sounding very uneasy. "We might end up...dead, Bethany. If we do die, I want you to know that I'm grateful for all the kindness you've shown me."

"We're not going to die," Bethany promised—at least she tried. *Maybe we will die. I don't know.*

"Let's go. We can run our mouths to each other later," Claude said as he grabbed Samantha's hand and hurried back downstairs. Bethany and Julie followed. Once downstairs, Claude made his way to the dining room door. To his relief more than shock, the door was hanging off its hinges. The force of the explosion had literally ripped the kitchen apart and torn through the dining room like a tidal wave of destruction. "Hold my rifle, Sam."

Bethany watched as Claude handed his wife a loaded rifle and then began working the dining room door free. The stacks of wooden chairs and tables that were pressed up against the backside of the door were now laying around the dining room like scattered body parts. Claude worked hard and fast, grunting and fussing under his breath as he pulled the dining room door free. The door was heavy, but the force of the explosion had disabled the door just enough to allow Claude victory. "All right…let's go," Claude ordered, pushing the dining room door off to his right side. The door hit the floor with a hard, loud *Whap*—an ugly dying sound that sent a chill down Bethany's spine.

This ski resort is a rotted crypt that's slowly starting to fall apart…no…not fall apart…decay. We have to get off this mountain before we all die. A sense of deep panic began to sprint through Bethany's heart. All feeling of control and order began to crumble like snow breaking loose from the side of a steep mountainside. *We have to get off this mountain…we have to….* Bethany began to breathe fast and hard…breaths associated with sudden panic and extreme anxiety. *I'm starting to lose control…just like I used to when my husband would holler at me and threaten to hurt me. I'm starting to lose control…*

Julie heard Bethany's breathing change. She spun around and, through the cold darkness, managed to spot a panicked face. "Love…deep breaths…it's all right."

"Nothing is ever going to be all right…the nightmares are never going to leave me…." Bethany felt her entire body begin to shake.

"Claude—" Samantha began to beg for her husband to help Bethany.

Claude quickly handed Julie his rifle and grabbed Bethany by her shoulders. "You listen to me," he said in a quick, firm tone, "you best get your mind together and stop panicking, do you hear me? You've already proved yourself to be a fighter. Don't start crumbling on me now, do you hear?"

"I...." *My husband never hit me...but once...he threw a perfume bottle across the room. The bottle crashed against the bedroom wall and broke...glass flew into the air...some of the glass cut my face...I had to get three stitches. I tried to act brave and sensible...functional...but deep down I was so scared...and...my marriage continued to...decay. It was all so pointless. I never won the battle...I never won.*

Claude threw his arms around Bethany and pulled the trembling woman into his chest. "I'm here," he whispered, dropping his voice into a tender whisper. There was no sense in trying to order Bethany to get her emotions together with a tough voice anymore. It was clear that Bethany needed a loving arm. "You've been brave. It's all right."

Bethany felt Claude wrap a pair of loving, safe, caring arms around her.

"I—" She struggled to speak but failed. *I'm caving in...stop it. Fight. You have to keep fighting!* Bethany screamed in her mind. *But why? Only to lose? You fought the killers in Snow Falls...and now look...you're going to die. What's the point in fighting? What's the point in trying to have courage and heart? The monsters always win!*

"Sometimes," Claude whispered in Bethany's ear, "it seems like giving up the fight makes the most sense. I guess at times life doesn't seem worth fighting for. But all we can keep doing is putting one foot in front of the other and pray the Good Lord above helps us make sense of what we're supposed to be doing. And let me tell you, even at my age, life still don't make sense. Sometimes I just look up at the sky and wonder what in the world I'm doing standing on God's earth."

"What are you doing?" Bethany managed to whisper.

"Oh, just what God intended for me to do," Claude whispered back, "love Him...fear Him...and do what's right in His sight...believe in His Son...and stay the course." Claude patted Bethany with a gentle hand. "That's mighty hard to do at times, but not impossible, so don't give up the fight, Bethany. Run your course."

Bethany lifted her head and peered into a face that she once found grumpy and hard. Claude Stewart was a man who hid his heart—but he was a man who had a heart, a very special heart that came out from behind a pair of gray clouds when needed and shined bright. "All right, Claude, I'll run my course...I'll try—"

"Help me!" a terrified voice screamed. "Someone help me...please!"

"Shelia!" Samantha yelled. "Claude, that's Shelia!"

"Ready to continue the fight?" Claude asked Bethany without showing too much alarm. Bethany drew in a deep breath and nodded. "Good girl. Let's go!" Claude took his rifle back from Julie and dashed into the dining room.

"Love?" Julie asked.

Bethany threw down the rag she was holding over her face. *Let my face bleed...let the blood fall. I have to keep fighting. No one said life was going to be a cakewalk. I...have to keep running my course, as hard as that might be. I can't break down and give up.* "I'm all right...just a temporary moment of...well, I'm all right. Let's go!"

Bethany charged into the dining room after Claude. Samantha and Julie took up the rear. "Help me...please!" Shelia's desperate voice pierced the dark air of the dining room.

Claude fought his way into a shattered kitchen that resembled a war zone. The kitchen looked as if ten tanks had fired on it all at once. "Sam, I need the light!" he yelled, screaming over piercing winds and heavy snow that was blowing into the kitchen. The entire back kitchen wall was missing. "Hurry!"

Samantha managed to get into the kitchen. She quickly

aimed the flashlight in her hand toward the walk-in freezer. Somehow the freezer was still standing completely intact. Part of the kitchen roof was laying in front of the freezer door. Claude tried to push the piece of collapsed roof free as heavy snow struck his face but failed. "You can't move it, Claude... stop trying," Samantha begged.

"Help me!" Shelia begged. "Oh please, help me!"

"Are you hurt?" Claude hollered.

"No, but—"

"Then stop your bellowing!" Claude roared. "We'll get you out when we can!"

"I don't think so!" Neil appeared where the back kitchen wall had once stood. Before anyone could act, Neil threw a flare into the destroyed kitchen and then stepped back. "Hands in the air!" he hollered, aiming a vicious rifle straight at Bethany. "One wrong move and I'll fill her full of bullets!"

The flare Neil threw into the kitchen began to glow so bright that everyone had to shield their eyes. All Bethany could see was a blinding light. *Stay the course...don't panic. Keep fighting...don't panic...remain functional.* Deep down inside of a terrified heart, Bethany wasn't so sure she could stay the course anymore. Perhaps, she confessed, the deadly monsters she had always feared had finally won a long and bitter war.

chapter eight

"I said get your hands in the air!" Neil yelled.

"Easy, boy!" Claude told Neil, speaking in a tough voice.

"Drop your rifle, old man! And you…I know you have a gun…get rid of it!" Neil yelled at Bethany.

Claude waited until the flare fizzled out before speaking. The brightness of the flare created a temporary blindness to the darkness. Claude struggled to see Neil but failed. It would take a minute for his eyes to adjust. "You gonna kill us?"

"I tried, but you're all still alive…and so is Shelia!" Neil couldn't believe that his victims were still alive. How? He had used every bit of remaining dynamite—dynamite that had once been used to create avalanches before the ski resort opened in order to protect happy skiers from future dangers —to blow the kitchen sky high. "Looks like I'm going to have to kill you the old-fashioned way!"

"Before you do…tell me one thing," Bethany said in a quick, sudden voice. "Who is Nathaniel Taylor?"

Neil froze. "What…did you say?" he asked, forcing his voice to carry over the screaming winds.

Bethany shielded her face from the sudden, sharp cold that was blasting into the destroyed kitchen. She felt heavy streams of blood running down the left side of her voice but ignored it. Her eyes worked to see Neil but failed. "We encountered a man we believe to be Nathaniel Taylor."

"What?" Neil's angry voice began to fill with panic. "No! No! No!" he yelled. "Shelia…you're going to pay for this! One way or the other!"

"What's wrong with you?" Claude snapped at Neil.

"I had it all planned out…all I had to do was…." Neil suddenly began to feel very hot, even though icy winds were cutting through his body like sharp razors. He threw up his left hand and ripped off a black ski mask. "I'll get you for this, Shelia! Wait and see." Neil turned and began to run on panicked legs, but then he suddenly stopped. Could he really leave his intended targets alive? Or maybe….

Neil thought in a desperate attempt to fight his way through a dangerous sea and reach ground—an irrational attempt that somehow made sense inside of his sick mind. "Look, maybe we can help each other?"

"What are you talking about?" Claude demanded.

Neil felt his heart racing so fast he felt as if he might pass out. If Nathaniel Taylor was on the scene…that meant he was a dead man. It was time to forget about playing the role of a killer. It was time to forget about the gold. Neil cared more about his life. "Look…in cabin number 4…Shelia's dad is in the cabin. He's alive. He's…the one who planned all this. He's waiting for me to kill you—"

Before Neil could say another word, a loud gunshot erupted. A bullet tore through the storm and entered Neil's back…and then grabbed his heart. Neil's body was thrown forward and crashed down into a splintered, destroyed kitchen floor. Anyone who might have seen Neil take the bullet would have known the man met death before his body hit the kitchen floor—or so it might have seemed.

"Is everyone all right?" John Richtore stepped into the kitchen on hurried legs.

Bethany shielded her eyes. "Mr. Richtore?"

"Yes, my dear, it's your dear old friend from the coffee shop," John said in a pleasant tone. "I'm so happy everyone is safe." John glanced around the kitchen. Neil had been foolish to blow up the kitchen. How would John be able to explain the explosion to the authorities when the time arrived? Destroying the rock gap was risky enough. Of course, John's paranoid, irrational thoughts didn't understand practical logic. John was living in a world of false illusions filled with poison deceit that blinded him from all truth. After hearing a violent explosion, he had quickly wandered out into the storm and hurried to the lodge—nearly freezing to death in the process. He spotted Neil throwing a flare into the kitchen…stood back…and listened. After hearing the name Nathaniel Taylor, John knew he had to act fast and change all of his original plans. Oh, how the wicked are never at peace. How the plans of the wicked never come to fruition. How the wicked are caught in their own snares and suffer the fate they planned for the innocent.

"I hope everyone is all right. I…seem to have arrived just at the right time."

Yes, you did, Bethany thought as her eyes painfully adjusted to the dark. *You showed up right on time. Coincidence? No.* Bethany drew in a deep breath. *All right, get a grip. You made it this far…you had a temporary breakdown…it happens. Get it together and think. If you're going to survive your new life, you're going to have to start getting tough. Life isn't going to sit back and feed you cotton candy. You're going to have to walk across a bed of hot coals and stop whining about it.* "Mr. Richtore, are you all right? We heard that you had been shot?" Bethany spoke in a voice that appeared to be deeply concerned.

"I'm all right, my dear. My daughter's husband was holding me captive. The man had a very devious plan in order." John stepped farther into the kitchen in order to escape the brunt of the razor-sharp winds that were tearing into him. "I can explain everything later...I heard the explosion...I was working to free myself from a set of ropes that were holding me to a chair. I managed to escape and dared the storm."

"I'm so grateful you're all right." Bethany dared to move forward. She threw out her hands. "Mr. Richtore, we have to get off this mountain," she begged, attempting to take John's gloved hands into her own. John was holding a gun that was currently aimed down at the kitchen floor. "We heard there was a radio. We need to call for help."

John wanted to step away from Bethany but didn't want to appear suspicious. He allowed the woman to take his free hand into her own. "Yes, there is a communication radio in the cabin I was being held hostage in. We can call the authorities, but first...I need to ask. As I approached and saw my daughter's husband threatening you...I thought I heard someone say the name Nathaniel Taylor?"

"Yes, I found that name written on a piece of paper in the attic crawl space your daughter hid in," Bethany confessed. "We encountered a man earlier...he managed to escape."

"I see." John gritted his teeth as his insane mind began to frantically search for desperate options. John believed he possessed a brilliant mind that no man or woman could outshine. Surely, he could...readjust...his plans and still manage to take possession of all the gold he hungered for and turn the ski resort into something majestic. Before John died, he would use the missing gold to erase a painful past and find...peace. What John didn't realize was that the wicked never had peace. "We do need to get off this mountain, then. My daughter...?"

"She's in the freezer...the freezer protected her from the explosion," Bethany explained. She squeezed John's hand. "You saved our lives, Mr. Richtore. Someday I'm going to buy you a hot cup of coffee and a warm donut. But right now, we need to contact the authorities. Please."

Claude heard something in Bethany's voice—a different key that clearly instructed a clever part he was now supposed to perform. "John, you showed up just at the right time. That crazy guy was going to kill us, but then he started babbling something about working together. Ain't never seen such craziness in all my life."

"Me, neither," Sam joined her husband.

Julie glanced toward the walk-in freezer. Surely Shelia was listening. "Sir, we need to get your daughter free."

"I wouldn't," John said, letting out a heavy sigh. "My daughter wanted me dead. She is not innocent, I'm afraid."

Inside the freezer, Shelia backed up against a cold wall and tried to think. She was trapped. There was no escape. All the woman could do was wait…or maybe there was a way to fight. "Nathaniel is on the mountain…he's going to kill you!" she screamed at John. "You know it!"

John tensed up. Yes. If Nathaniel Taylor was on the mountain, the man most certainly would kill him—kill everyone. It seemed that Shelia had managed to pull a hidden card from her sleeve without being seen. The only thought that allowed John to remain in place was the fact that he was still alive. Surely if Nathaniel Taylor was on the mountain, the man would have killed everyone within a matter of hours. Nathaniel Taylor was a ruthless killer. "See what I mean?" John pretended to speak in a sorrowful voice. "My own daughter. My own daughter—"

"Wanted you dead?" a voice asked.

Bethany looked past John just in time to see a shadowy figure appear. Her eyes were slowly adjusting to the dark again, allowing certain shapes and figures to appear. She felt John's body turn stiff and freeze up. "Mr. Taylor?"

Brad Cunningham shook his head no. "Nathaniel Taylor is currently handcuffed inside of a snowcat. He's also currently taking a very long sleep. Being hit in the head with the butt of a rifle can do that." Brad popped on a small pen light that possessed a very powerful beam. "My name is Special Agent Brad Cunningham. Sorry I arrived late to the show. I did arrive in time to see Nathaniel Taylor sneaking around in the storm."

"You're a cop?" Claude called out.

"I work for the FBI," Brad informed Claude, speaking over the screaming winds.

Bethany squinted her eyes and tried to see Brad. All she saw was a man wearing black gear and a black ski mask. *If I'm not mistaken...and my eyes are still suffering from the brightness of that awful flare...the man standing in the storm is about the same height as the man Claude and I shot at...he's built about the same way too.*

"Agent Cunningham, two people are dead. There's a woman trapped in the freezer. Please. We need help...right, Claude?" Claude quickly began to speak, running interference for Bethany. Bethany began easing her hand over to the gun John was holding...unseen and unheard. "Don't move," she whispered to John, just low enough for Brad not to hear as Claude ran interference. "No more games. I know you're a killer...but the man standing behind us will kill us where we stand. If you want to live, do as I say."

"That's Nathaniel Taylor," John hissed under his breath.

"I know." Bethany drew in a deep breath. *The man standing over there is going to kill us. It's now or never. I have to act. I may not have this crime scene figured out...I may not be able to match Sarah's detective skills...and I even had a breakdown for a minute... but I have to keep fighting. For better or worse...in this life, as horribly scary...painful...and confusing as life is...a woman has no other choice but to keep fighting or give up. I don't want to give up and end up like Shelia Pacemore.* "When I yell, you hit the floor...I'll deal with you later."

"The gold is all mine, do you hear?" John hissed as Claude continued to blab off his mouth, fussing about his snowcat having no gas. "I'll have my gold...no one will stop me."

Shelia heard Claude gabbing away. Claude was a man of few words. From what Shelia knew of the man—which wasn't much—Claude wasn't a talker. Something was fishy. But what? Shelia was standing in the dark. All she could do was listen. "That old man is up to something," Shelia whispered as cold sweat ran down her face. She was desperate for a hit…nearly out of her wind with hunger for her drug of choice. Surely Nathaniel would have saved her. "I can't stand it anymore…." Shelia closed her eyes—and feeling her mind finally collapse into a dark, bottomless, abyss, she screamed: "Kill them, Nathaniel! Kill them! Kill them all!"

"Now! Get down!" Bethany hollered at John as she tore the gun the old man was holding from his hand. John dove down onto the floor as Bethany tore his gun free with a powerful hand.

Nathaniel was wearing a pair of night vision goggles. He clearly saw Bethany snatch a gun out of John's hands. He quickly raised a high-powered rifle into the air and aimed at Bethany with his firing finger firmly pressed on a deadly trigger. Bethany squeezed a hard trigger three times as she dropped down onto her one knee. Three hungry bullets erupted from the gun and growled at Nathaniel just as Nathaniel fired off one single shot at Bethany. Nathaniel was prepared to eat a few bullets. He was wearing a military-designed bulletproof vest that could withstand a few sissy bullets.

The bullet Nathaniel fired at Bethany missed its target and tore into a shattered wall mere inches away from Julie. The three bullets Bethany fired at Nathaniel flew high…and struck a deadly target right in the face. Nathaniel felt his head snap back on his shoulders as three hard punches that came in the form of deadly bullets knocked his life into a deep grave.

Claude didn't waste a second. He threw his rifle into a firing position. "Sam…light!" he yelled and charged forward toward Nathaniel's body. Samantha gave her husband light and watched as the brave man stepped over a dead body.

"Is he dead?" Bethany asked in a voice that sounded very shaky.

Claude bent down and examined Nathaniel's face. It didn't take him but a second to see that the man was deader than a doornail. "You did good!" he called out in a triumphant voice.

Bethany began to stand up but stopped when a painful moan left Neil's mouth. "No!" John cried out in rage. "I shot him! He's dead!" John tried to stand up and make a run for it, but Samantha threw out a quick hand and slapped the old man sideways. John stumbled back down onto the floor… hitting his head on a broken piece of the wood in the process…and from there…it was lights out.

"Anyone else ready to go home?" Julie asked and then simply dropped her shoulders. "You Americans are crazy creatures. Have a cup of relaxing tea and a crumpet some time."

Bethany, Samantha, and Claude all let out a shaky, exhausted laugh at the same time. What else could they do trapped in a deadly storm that was filled with hungry killers? *It's time to go home. It's time to leave this mountain…this crypt… and go home.* Bethany bowed her head and closed her eyes. *Alive…alive to live another day. For better or worse…*

"All their stories are completely different," Bethany said in a calm voice as she sipped on a hot cup of coffee. "Shelia…her husband…the old man…all three of them have different stories that don't make sense. All I can honestly suggest is that each of them created a deadly scheme in their minds that they believed would work."

"Stupid blokes," Amanda Hardcastle fussed up a storm.

"You two could have been killed!" Amanda turned her attention to her cousin Julie. "From now on, you're not leaving my sight." Amanda's British accent was dipping into deep water. Being angry caused a flood to appear.

Julie folded her arms over a brown and green dress. "Amanda, love, I don't have a problem in the world with that."

Sarah Spencer took a minute to soak in everything Bethany had told her. Bethany was sitting calmly before a warm fire in a comfortable recliner. It seemed that the woman was at peace, but Sarah knew better. "Amanda, will you take Julie to O'Mally's? We're expecting a shipment of food today…and…don't eat all the food, please."

Amanda shoved her hands into the pockets of a thick white winter coat. "Come on, Julie. We have work to do…and don't leave my sight." Amanda looked at Bethany. "Love, from what Julie told me, you really saved the day up on that mountain. You're quite amazing." Amanda offered a loving smile and then dragged Julie over to a wooden coatrack. "Get your coat on."

"Yes, Amanda." Julie shot Bethany a desperate smile. "I'll be with the warden if you need me."

"Okay." Bethany laughed a little as she watched Amanda drag Julie out into a soft falling snow.

Sarah bit down on her lower lip, removed a green winter coat, and sat down on a brown couch. "The website I located for you was created eight days before Mr. Richtore visited Snow Falls. The website was created by a company in Arizona."

"Mandy Pacemore?" Bethany asked.

"Yes," Sarah nodded.

Bethany brushed at her brown sweater and stood up. She walked over to a warm fire and grew silent for a few minutes. Sarah allowed the silence. "From what I was able to gather, Sarah, a paranoid old man was the one who tricked me into traveling up to that awful ski lodge. He had Mandy Pacemore pretend to be Shelia Vermont."

"There's more to Mandy Pacemore than people realize," Sarah informed Bethany. "But we'll talk about that later." Sarah carefully studied Bethany as the woman warmed her hands over a soft fire. "You're having a hard time, aren't you?" she asked.

Bethany knew there was no point in pretending that she didn't know what Sarah meant. "Yes," she offered a clear and honest answer. "Sometimes I feel like I'm going out of my mind. I can't seem to reconcile my past with the present...or the future. I still feel trapped in a dark cage."

"Believe it or not, I understand how you feel."

Bethany turned to face Sarah. She spotted a beautiful, brilliant woman that she admired and respected. "Oh Sarah, if you had been trapped at that ski lodge, you would have figured out the crime scene in a matter of minutes and had all the bad guys under lock and key. Me? I fumbled around so badly that I'm shocked I didn't get anyone killed...I also nearly had a mental breakdown." A sad, defeated laugh left Bethany's lips. "I wonder why I keep fighting."

"According to Claude and Samantha Stewart, you saved everyone's life from a man who was a known assassin." Sarah stood up and approached Bethany. "Mr. and Mrs. Stewart spoke very highly of your actions."

Bethany sighed. "Claude and Samantha are in Fairbanks fussing with their son-in-law. Claude has finally agreed to let his hunting lodge be turned into a marriage retreat...but he's still putting up a fuss. I think Samantha is happy. They're both very wonderful people."

"Who have made it very clear that they both love you and Julie," Sarah pointed out.

"Well...we love them too. Claude and Samantha are a permanent part of my life now." Bethany looked into Sarah's caring eyes. She spotted a true friend. "You know, Sarah, the entire time I was trapped at the ski resort, I kept reminding myself to think like you…act like you…be as brave as you."

"Bethany, this might come as a shock to you, but I get scared…I never have anything figured out…I always bump into dead ends…and I've come close to dying more times than I care to admit." Sarah moved past Bethany and stood in front of an inviting fireplace. "I still have nightmares, and each day is a battle for me. Most of the time I simply…wing it."

"Really?" Bethany asked in a shocked voice. "But Sarah, you always seem so—"

"Tough? Like a woman who has it all together?" Sarah asked. Bethany nodded. "Bethany, I wish that were true. As far as being a mother to Little Sarah and being a wife to Conrad…yes, I have it together. But as far as in here"—Sarah tapped the side of her head—"inside of my mind…well, honey, I'm always running from shadows."

"Really?"

Sarah stared into soft, flowing flames. "Julie and I had a talk two days ago—a private talk. She went into detail about everything that happened at the ski resort. Julie told me everything that happened and, more importantly, how you acted and what you did."

"Julie paints me as some type of hero when I'm not—"

"No, you're not a hero, and neither am I," Sarah gently cut Bethany off. "You were trapped in a bad situation and did what you had to do to survive. That's all anyone can do, Bethany. But the fact is, you didn't give up the fight." Sarah slowly folded her arms. "The piece of paper you found with the name of Nathaniel Taylor written on it also contained four numbers you assumed belonged to a telephone number. The numbers were, in fact, a password that unlocked a communication radio. What if you wouldn't have dared to investigate the attic crawl space? How would you have called out for help?"

"I suppose...eventually we would have located the snowcat Nathaniel Taylor used to reach the ski resort," Bethany offered.

"Maybe...." Sarah finally turned to face Bethany. "Nathaniel Taylor didn't immediately strike because he wasn't certain who you or Julie were...at least that's according to a tape recording that was found on a tape recorder hidden in Nathaniel Taylor's coat pocket." Sarah looked deeply into Bethany's eyes. "As confusing as John Richtore's confession is...and I've heard far more irrational testimonies, trust me...by tricking you and Julie into traveling to the ski resort, the man actually saved his own life. Because he's alive, the police have managed to gain further confessions from him that involve drugs and guns that are connected to some very bad people."

"Why are you telling me these things, Sarah?" Bethany asked.

"Because life will never make sense, Bethany," Sarah stressed. "We're never going to have the bad guys figured out. We're never going to conquer a crime scene. We're never going to truly understand the mind of a killer. We're never going to be able to chase away the shadows. Life is connected to a network of horrible mazes that we'll never find our way through. All we can do is take one day at a time and do the best we can with what God, out of His mercy, gives us."

"That's easier said than done." Bethany walked back to her recliner and sat down. "Tomorrow doesn't seem too inviting."

"Honey, look where you're sitting."

"In my recliner—" Bethany began to answer.

"In your home, alive...safe and sound," Sarah pressed and then approached Bethany. "You suffered through years of a bad marriage and two very dangerous murder cases. But yet, here you sit." Sarah reached down and took Bethany's hand. "Tomorrow may not seem very inviting, but tomorrow will come…and what will Bethany Lights do? Give up or face tomorrow with a brave face?"

"I suppose…I'll keep running the race." Bethany looked up into Sarah's eyes. "I'll never truly figure out what happened up at the ski resort, will I?"

"I doubt it," Sarah confessed. "You might draw a few confident conclusions, but you'll never have a final answer that soothes your mind." Sarah shook her head. "I have countless unsettled cases running around in the back room of my mind."

"I suppose you're right." Bethany looked down at her hands. "The ski resort has been marked off limits by the state. Not that the state of Alaska can enforce that rule. I seriously doubt if the state is going to post year-round guards to patrol the ski resort."

"Probably not. And it's my guess there will be a lot of foolish people that will venture up to the ski resort searching for gold." Sarah walked back to the warm couch and sat down. "Maybe there is gold up there? Mr. Richtore and his daughter refused to talk about the gold. It's like you said, Bethany, everyone's story is different and filled with confusing twists and turns that don't really make sense to a practical mind."

"It does sound insane, doesn't it?" Bethany asked. "Betrayal…lies…drugs…murder…all twisted into the minds of four people who planned to kill each other."

"Mandy Pacemore was intending to kill Mr. Richtore. She assumed she was manipulating the old man…well, that's another twist in the maze that a dead woman will never solve." Sarah leaned back on the couch she was sitting on and folded her hands over her knee. "Life never ceases to amaze me, Bethany. While we're sitting here…at this very moment, some killer is out there planning to strike…a killer that may be dangerously brilliant or dangerously anxious…like the killers you encountered on Ice Mountain."

Before Bethany could respond, someone knocked on the cabin door. Bethany stiffened some. "Who is it?"

"Your mother!" a fussy voice hollered.

"Mother?" Bethany nearly wet her pants. She jumped to her feet and ran to the front door. Sarah watched as Bethany yanked the front door open and greeted a short woman wearing a very angry face. "Mother?"

"Don't you mother me!" Bethany's mother snapped, charging past her daughter. "The FBI called me. Do you want to know why the FBI called me? I'll tell you why the FBI called me! The FBI called me because they wanted to know all about you because it seems my daughter was involved with a killing!"

Sarah tucked her head down as Bethany's mother ripped a gray snow hat off her head, revealing a deep set of gray hair that matched a gray winter coat. It was clear that Bethany's mother was dressed for war. "Maybe I should go—"

"No...uh, stay, Sarah. Please. I'll make coffee and...I baked a cake," Bethany began to whimper.

"Yes, some coffee would be nice. You!" Bethany's mother pointed at Sarah. "Coffee. One sugar. Very little creamer. Go."

"Yes, ma'am." Sarah shot to her feet and hurried away, leaving poor Bethany alone with a very angry woman.

"Mother, this situation isn't what you think—"

"A woman was killed...and according to the FBI you shot an...dare I say it, Bethany...oh, have mercy on my poor heart...an assassin! An assassin! Your poor daddy must be taking an ocean of aspirin in Heaven right now." Bethany's mother plopped down on the warm couch. "What in the world were you thinking? Oh...never mind. You are to pack your belongings. I've come to take you back to North Carolina after I rest."

Life is filled with a network of mazes that we will never figure out...right now there is a killer preparing to strike...all we can do is take it one day at a time and use the gifts God gives us... Sarah's voice began whispering in Bethany's ear. She looked down into her mother's face. Suddenly a strange calmness entered her heart that really didn't make any sense.

"Mother, I entertained the idea of moving to North Carolina, but Alaska is my home now." Bethany sat down next to her mother. She took the woman's hand with a gentle love. "What happened up on Ice Mountain wasn't my fault. I didn't plan to encounter the situation I did. I was forced to act...and I admit, that I had a very difficult time because...my life still feels as if it's in shambles. But here I am."

Bethany's mother dared to look into a set of soft, pleading eyes that were filled with a pain she had never witnessed before—a pain that whispered up from a deep hole created by years of verbal and mental abuse. Instead of insisting that Bethany change her mind and return to North Carolina, Bethany's mother suddenly dropped her head. "I can't stand to look into your eyes any longer."

Tears began to drip from the eyes of the sorrowful woman. "Mother?" Bethany asked, watching her mother begin to cry.

"I knew your husband was abusing you...so did your daddy. But what could we do? He wasn't physically hitting you. And...our family...you understand how precious the family reputation is, Bethany. How many people would have pounced all over your divorce? And now...your eyes...."

Bethany carefully slipped an arm around her mother. "Maybe we can talk...for once?" she asked in a hopeful voice as tears began to fall from her own eyes. "I need my mother... I always have. I wish...I could have come to you and Daddy...."

"Oh Bethany!" Bethany's mother threw her arms around her daughter as large, painful, sobbing tears left her eyes. "I'm here...I'm so sorry...I can't stand to look into your eyes."

All Bethany could do was hold her crying mother. *Life is filled with a network of confusing mazes that we will never figure out...and this is one of those mazes. From being trapped at a deadly ski resort that felt like a cold morgue to holding my crying mother. Oh Lord, when does the healing begin? When does the light arrive?*

Bethany didn't have an answer to many of the questions whispering in her heart. All she could do was hold her mother. Sarah, who was watching from a distance, simply smiled and faded away into the distance.

"You're going to be all right, Bethany Lights. In time, you're going to be all right. You have a very difficult battle ahead of you, but in the end…just like me…you're going to be just fine. I promise."

As Bethany held her crying mother, Julie's cell phone rang far away. Julie answered the call, listened to a voice speak, and then put her cell phone away. When Amanda asked if everything was all right, all Julie could say was "It looks like Bethany and I are going to take another holiday…." Amanda looked into her cousin's face. Something was horribly wrong…horribly wrong.

A killer was waiting in the darkness…waiting to strike.

Yes. Life was certainly full of a network of confusing mazes that Bethany Lights was going to be forced to face.

more from wendy

Alaska Cozy Mystery Series

Maple Hills Cozy Series

Sweeetfern Harbor Cozy Series

Sweet Peach Cozy Series

Sweet Shop Cozy Series

Twin Berry Bakery Series

about wendy meadows

Wendy Meadows is a USA Today bestselling author whose stories showcase women sleuths. To date, she has published dozens of books, which include her popular Sweetfern Harbor series, Sweet Peach Bakery series, and Alaska Cozy series, to name a few. She lives in the "Granite State" with her husband, two sons, two mini pigs and a lovable Labradoodle.

Join Wendy's newsletter to stay up-to-date with new releases. As a subscriber, you'll also get BLACKVINE MANOR, the complete series, for FREE!

Join Wendy's Newsletter Here
wendymeadows.com/cozy